KIM HARRISO

This special signed edition
is limited to **1500** numbered copies
and **26** lettered copies.

This is copy 919.

Perfunctory Affection

Perfunctory Affection

KIM HARRISON

SUBTERRANEAN PRESS 2019

First Edition

ISBN
978-1-59606-896-4

Subterranean Press
PO Box 190106
Burton, MI 48519

subterraneanpress.com

Manufactured in the United States of America

For Tim

Acknowledgments

Many thanks to my agent Jennifer Jackson for her steadfast belief, and Yanni Kuznia at Subterranean Press for her always cheerful understanding with my questions.

One

She'd known what was real before Dr. Jillium increased her meds. Of that Meg was certain. Beyond that, nothing was sure.

The campus's cramped roads had become black with night, and the sudden right angles made her headlights almost useless as she drove to the hospital. What Haley said couldn't be true. Meg hadn't done those things. How could she? It had been Austin.

Confusion-born tears started, and the car threatened to stall as she took a corner too tight.

Austin had been there. Haley was lying. She was a mean, spiteful bitch who'd pretended to like her for her own sadistic mind games. Meg should've known it was too good to be true that Haley actually *liked* her. People as perfect as Haley didn't make friends with basket cases like her. Rorry was even worse, pretending to protect her from

Austin when all Rorry was doing was protecting Haley's "investment."

"I'm a plaything to them. A toy." Wiping her eyes, she bounced over the road bumps, struggling not to cry from the heartache of being used. "I can't believe I painted a picture for him. Son of a bitch. Son of a bitch!"

The canvas was beside her where Austin once sat, its lines lost in the darkness. Throwing it away wasn't an option. It was her best work, the beginning of something totally new, and now, she'd think of him every time she looked at it.

"Damn him. Damn them both," she whispered. Frustrated, Meg hit the dash, and her hand began to bleed again through the bandage. Meg stared at the slick sheen leaking out, her panic rising anew. Was it really bleeding or just an illusion? Had she cut her hand or burned it?

"I hate this car," she said softly, and then louder, when she realized she'd missed the turn and was headed into the nearby park, "I hate this car! Why am I even driving this car!"

Suddenly her headlights gleamed on the ragged silhouette of a man in the road, waving at her to stop. It was Christopher, and gasping, Meg spun the wheel to avoid him. That damned little dog of his jerked his lead free and ran away, but Christopher froze in fear. Panicking, Meg hit the gas instead of the brake.

With a sickening lurch, the car angled off the road and onto the open grass toward the trees. Meg shrieked,

Perfunctory Affection

paralyzed as the memory of her accident rose up, thick and smothering. The impact of the curb bounced her head into the wheel, and dazed, she could do nothing but cross her arms over her face as the trees flashed past bright with light. With a jaw-snapping thud, the car ran into a tree and stalled.

For three seconds, Meg didn't move, her breath a harsh rasp as she remembered where she was. There'd been no airbag to cushion her this time, and the taste of blood slicked her teeth. Dazed, she looked at the empty seat beside her, relief pushing out the fear. It wasn't one of her nightmares. It was real and she was okay. Austin wasn't here, his hand mangled and his leg nearly severed at the hip by a metal fence support. There was only a canvas lying on the floor, one that would haunt her for the rest of her life.

"I hate this car," she whispered, wishing she'd gotten the airbag replaced along with the passenger side door. But it hadn't seemed to matter if she wasn't going to drive the thing.

Then Christopher banged on the window, and she jumped, shrieking.

"You have to kill them!" he shouted through the window, and Meg scrambled to the other side of the car and got out in a panic.

"Stay away from me!" she exclaimed as she reached back in for her purse, backing away from him as he came around the car. "You're crazy. Crazy!"

"Like hell I am," he growled, and she gasped as he grabbed her arm. "It's not too late. Come with me to the fountain. They need moving water. That's how they get here. They haven't left. Help me. We have to kill them both or you'll never know what's real again. Don't let them take you. Perfection isn't real. *They* aren't real!"

If they aren't real, then why do you want to kill them? she thought, but there was no logic to crazy. "Get away from me!" Meg wedged his hand off her. Shoving him back, she began to run to the hospital. She had to talk to Dr. Jillium, stand in front of her and find out what was real and what wasn't, because if Perfection wasn't an illusion, then what she'd done wasn't either.

Two

Three days previous

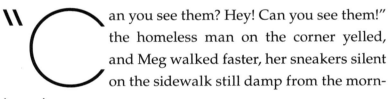an you see them? Hey! Can you see them!" the homeless man on the corner yelled, and Meg walked faster, her sneakers silent on the sidewalk still damp from the morning rain.

"It's just a crazy old man walking his dog, Meg," she chided herself. Her anxiety, though probably warranted this time, was a comfortable sweater, familiar and worn, and oh so pleasant when life closed in—a bad habit that Dr. Jillium was trying to convince her she didn't need. Meg had her doubts. It was her anxiety that kept her going when her art failed to remind her she was alive.

"If you can't see them, it's not too late!" the man shouted again, and Meg hunched deeper into her long, wool sweater coat.

Kim Harrison

The college-town street was busy with lunch hour traffic. It wound a parched path between ragged sorority houses and low-slung, seventies-modern offsite apartments, the narrow sidewalk hemmed by sun-starved grass, ancient oaks, and old wisteria slowly strangling the trees that gave them life. Timing the cars, Meg crossed the street, her pace quickening when the man's dog barked at her.

"Nasty little ankle biter," she whispered as she held her purse closer, but the tightness in her chest had eased. Dr. Jillium's office was in the three-story apartment building just up the street. The new medication that her psychiatrist had given her to try last week had done nothing to alleviate her oft-times crippling anxiety made worse by Austin's conviction that talking would make it all better. But in all fairness, it had only been a trial dose to see how her body tolerated the experimental drug. Today she'd find out if she'd get the full course and join her psychiatrist's ongoing research—and Meg was anxious about that too.

Her pulse quickened as it always did as she rose up the three stone steps and rang the buzzer. "It's me, Dr. J," she said, leaning in toward the speaker and fidgeting with her necklace. Her mother had given the length of sterling silver to her after she graduated from art school; the tiny palette inset with precious stones for blobs of color was a show of pride and unconditional love. It and the car were all Meg had left apart from the interest she lived on from

14

the veritable fortune she'd never known her mother had possessed until she was gone.

The harsh buzzing of the door lock shocked through Meg and made her jump. "Hi Meg," Dr. Jillium said through the speaker, her high voice cheerful. "Come on up. Door is unlocked."

As always, Meg thought, but the repetition was comforting. Shoulders easing, Meg pulled the heavy glass door open, stressing over her wet footprints on the pastel-toned vintage floor tile. Taking large steps to minimize the mess, Meg walked on only the black squares to get past the old-fashioned mail boxes and to the old oak steps.

She rose up the two flights fast, glancing at the elegant brass nameplate for reassurance before knocking once and entering. DR. JANICE JILLIUM. It was the sole indication that this was an office rather than a residence. The small nod to privacy had made it easier for Meg to come that first difficult day. She wasn't embarrassed about seeing a therapist to help her with her grief over her mother's death, but there was no need to advertize it to her students.

"Hi, Dr. J. It's me," Meg said softly as she came in and shut the door, taking her sweater coat off as she scanned the open-floor apartment turned psychiatrist office. Wide picture windows looked out onto the wet quad, the waiting area with its outdated magazines arranged to take in the view of the campus's clock tower. The art building where

Kim Harrison

Meg taught was visible behind the tops of the oak trees, and Meg curled her fingers under her palms when she noticed she still had paint under her fingernails.

The small kitchen was dark, the bare counters and shelves holding little more than instant coffee and colorful mugs. The heart of the home had been reduced to a glorified coffee station, which had always given Meg a faint unease. There was a desk in the corner, but no receptionist. She'd never seen any other patient, either, but Dr. Jillium valued her patients privacy, and the university wasn't so large that sheer numbers would grant that without careful timing of appointments.

"Did you get caught in the rain?" Dr. Jillium's voice came from the open door that led to the inner office, and Meg hung her sweater beside Dr. Jillium's rain slicker on the hat rack. Reluctant to step off the rug beside the door, Meg continued to wipe her feet.

"No," she finally said. "The sidewalks are still wet, though."

Dr. Jillium came out of her office in a clicking of low heels, the early-forties, slim woman looking collected and comfortable in the gray skirt and white blouse that was slowly becoming the professional woman's uniform, the classy look mimicking the functionality of a man's suit. "Aren't you lucky. It was coming down cats and dogs only a few minutes ago," she said pleasantly as she touched her

Perfunctory
Af**fection**

tightly bound cornrows and headed into the abandoned kitchen. Meg envied her oblivious grace, her ancestry making her exotic and graceful. "I know you have a walk. You work today, don't you?"

"After our appointment." Face to face with her therapist's collected polish, Meg was suddenly conscious of her casual sneakers, ankle-length skirt and white blouse. It looked as if she'd raided her mother's closet, but it did say *teacher* among the students predominant jeans and T-shirts. Her lightly curling brown hair, brown eyes, and slight build made her blend in, otherwise.

"Classes just started up," Meg said as she looked out the large window. "I have a Monday, Wednesday, and Friday this semester."

Dr. Jillium turned from having taken two mugs from behind the glass-paneled cupboard. "How's that going?"

Meg shrugged, not wanting to bring up the nameless panic that had gripped her in the hall two days ago, rising up to swamp her before she beat it back. *Small victories lead to vanquished fears.* She was tired of being afraid of nothing. "Okay. I've got a full class and a waiting list." Her painting had been a godsend, her run-of-the-mill oils somehow evolving into a dramatic expression while she struggled with her mother's death. For her art she would stretch herself beyond her comfort zone—and Dr. Jillium wasn't above utilizing that fact to her advantage.

Kim Harrison

The dim light in the kitchen glinted dully on Dr. Jillium's smile as she handed Meg her usual slate-gray mug, full of straight black coffee, then clinked it to her milk-laden brew in salute. "Word gets around. Everyone wants to learn to catch the light the way you do."

The porcelain was warming even as she held it, and Meg nodded, thinking it was more about defining the negative space than highlighting the light, but even she could tell her reputation was growing. "Double-edged sword," Meg said sourly. Teaching was supposed to have been an easy way to get Dr. Jillium off her case about reinforcing her positive social interaction, but five students had turned into fifteen unsettlingly quick. Worse, her university-based show last year had done extremely well. Austin hadn't said a word about her fleeing the champagne-and-cheese-laced accolades after only fifteen minutes, but she knew he was disappointed. *For me, not in me,* Meg thought, not knowing what she'd do without Austin's steady presence in her life.

"Well, come on in," Dr. Jillium said as she headed for the bright rectangle of her office door. "I want to assess how you've been handling the Fitrecepon before we go too much further."

A quiver of excitement made her hands tremble, and Meg took a steadying breath, not knowing what to do with the rare emotion. The office wasn't bright today due to the overcast skies, but Dr. Jillium pulled the sheers anyway to help instill a deeper feeling of privacy. A cool breath of air slipped over Meg, and she relaxed in the faint sound of the ever-present air conditioner. Dr. Jillium had allergies and the windows didn't open.

A well-organized desk was set to overlook the quad. Meg rarely saw Dr. Jillium at it, but it was obvious this was where she worked. *This* was where Dr. Jillium's heart resided, valuing ordered pages instead of flour and eggs, a laptop instead of a stove and cookbooks—and that suited the tall, graceful, dark-skinned woman very well. Meg had always imagined that the antique, frosted-glass-door desiccator behind the desk held Dr. Jillium's experimental anti-anxiety drugs, but she'd never seen it open. A fern sat atop the old cabinet to catch the light. Another fern sat in the center of the narrow coffee table surrounded by a couch and several identical chairs.

The arrangement was meant to evoke a comfortable living room, the focal point being a gas-log fireplace instead of the usual TV, and, coffee in hand, Meg took her usual chair beside the never-lit fireplace, set her purse beside her, sipped her coffee, and eased back. Again, a faint feeling of eagerness coursed through her, just the hint of it feeling like springtime after a devastating winter. "I haven't noticed anything different," she said, and Dr. Jillium smiled as she sat across from her in a chair. Both women shunned the couch as a matter of tradition.

"That's good." Eyes down, Dr. Jillium powered up her tablet to take notes with. "The changes Fitrecepon creates in your brain are permanent, so we want to make sure they are the right ones. I didn't give you enough Fitrecepon to visibly impact your moods, just your nervous system. We've run into the occasional detrimental side effects in the past, and I don't want to make things more difficult when you're already making good progress."

Meg snorted her opinion, gaining a one-eyebrow look from Dr. Jillium. Meg still couldn't get behind the wheel of her car without palpitations, and meeting new people gave her the sweats. Finding a new grocery store when her local mom-and-pop had closed had been a three-week night-mare. But on the positive side, she did still have Austin, even if their relationship was sketchy at the moment. She'd been able to handle a job again, too, managing to work with new students every year. That she might be able to drive without fear or go the movies without freaking out when someone sat behind her sounded like heaven.

"So," Dr. Jillium prompted, stylus at the ready. "How was your week? Have you thought about your and Austin's relationship?"

Meg's eyes darted to the pinky ring Austin had given her three years ago after her mother had died. Her hand fisted, and she forced her gaze up to the windows beyond Dr. Jillium's silhouette. The ring was silver so she wouldn't confuse it with a proposal—if it fitting on her pinky hadn't been enough of a clue. "I'm warming up to it," she said to avoid telling her he'd up and moved out. It was no consolation that his things were still there, a constant reminder of how stupid she'd been. He said it wasn't her, that he was just going to spend a few days across campus until things got sorted out, but Meg could tell he was tired of their bickering and exhausted from dealing with her restless sleep. Nightmares of the car accident that had left him with a soft limp and limited use of his right hand still haunted her sleep.

"Mmmm-hum," Dr. Jillium murmured, making a notation. "How about your goal of getting out to the mall during the busy hours?"

Meg shrugged. She'd had her coat on and had been on her way, but then it had started to rain, and knowing that she'd have to take the bus made her palms sweat and her chest hurt. It had been easier to wait until after eight, just before the stores closed and there weren't so many people. "Sort of," she admitted when Dr. Jillium waited. "I'm hoping that this new medication will make things easier."

"This is not a magic pill," the woman said evenly, but Meg could tell she was cross. "You still have to exert yourself. You're retraining your brain to disengage from the fight or flight response. I know it's hard, Meg."

"Sometimes I wonder," Meg muttered from around a sip of coffee, then relented. "I'm tired of being afraid," she said,

Kim Harrison

frustration making her voice harsher than she intended. "I don't want a magic pill. I just want to be normal."

Expression carefully placid, Dr. Jillium swiped through her tablet. "There are no right or wrong answers to this, so don't try to feed me what you think I want. Okay?"

Meg sat up, set down her coffee, and crossed her knees. She wanted to be normal so bad, it ached.

Dr. Jillium cleared her throat. "Have your sleep patterns changed this week? Any night disturbances? Sleepwalking? Napping in the middle of the day or possibly waking up and having forgotten you fell asleep?"

"No," Meg said immediately. "No napping, but I've always woken up in the middle of the night." Actually, it was more like insomnia, her mind not letting her fall asleep as it went over what she could have done to keep Austin from leaving, what she ought to have said, was she making a mistake, what could she do to get him back, and did she even want him back. Her mind was inventive in its endless things to worry about.

"So, that would be a no on changing sleep patterns," Dr. Jillium said as she wrote that down. "How about eating? Does everything taste as it's supposed to?" Meg stared blankly, and Dr. Jillium added, "Is there anything you liked and now can't stand? Any new cravings you can't satisfy?"

"Oh. No," Meg quickly assured her. Her mac and cheese was as mac and cheesy as always, and Ben and Jerry's was

22

as consoling as ever after midnight. If not for having to walk everywhere, she'd be ten pounds heavier.

"Skin irritations?" Dr. Jillium questioned. "Any new rashes from detergent or fabrics?"

"Ah, no." Meg shook her head, surprised. These were detrimental side effects? They sounded like mere inconveniences compared to the ongoing hell her day-to-day was.

Dr. Jillium looked up from her tablet, stylus at rest. "I want you to think about your encounters this past week. Is your anxiety better, worse, or about the same? In particular, are you having trouble with situations that you know are nonthreatening but feel as such?"

Meg turned her lower lip in as she thought about the homeless man and his tiny dog on the corner. Flushing, she decided that was normal. For her. "Dr. J, I have fifteen new students that make my stomach cramp every time I walk into my classroom. But I'm not puking after class like I did last semester, so you can make what you want of that."

A smile crinkled the corners of Dr. Jillium's eyes. "I'd say that's a big no as well. I understand your frustration, but Meg, you really are improving."

Meg sighed, and Dr. Jillium's smile widened. Progress? Maybe, but it was too slow for Meg. Maybe too slow to save her relationship with Austin, and definitely too slow for her liking. "I'm tired of being afraid," Meg said, her eyes down as she laid her soul bare. "I *want* to be outgoing and happy again. I want to know I'll be able to go to dinner or a concert without leaving halfway through because of the walls closing in or a nameless fear I can't see."

Meg looked up at Dr. Jillium's silence, surprised at the sympathy there. "I'm tired of having to look at Austin and see his disappointment as he tells me it's okay," she added softly. "He's tired of never seeing the end of a movie or ball game, and I'm tired of the guilt when he leaves with me. You see progress, but I'm still living in the same hell I have been the last three years, and I'm *tired* of fighting for every last scrap of normal life," Meg said, not caring that her tone was bordering on self pity. "I feel that if I stop, I'll slide right back where I was, and I can't keep fighting. Please. I want to try this."

Dr. Jillium was silent for a moment, and then, motions holding a balanced grace, she set the tablet on the table. There were little checked boxes, and Meg's pulse quickened when Dr. Jillium hit an icon on the screen, and across the room, the printer hummed to life.

"You seem to be handling the initializing dose just fine," Dr. Jillium said as she stood. "I see no reason not to put you on a therapeutic level. Did you get the medical waiver signed and notarized?"

Meg exhaled, her breath shaking in her. "Yes," she said as she reached for her purse and found it. After two days spent scraping her courage together to go into the bank,

Perfunctory
Af**fection**

Austin had told her there was a notary at the realtor office downtown. There'd only been one person to deal with instead of a bank full, and Austin had offered to pay the fee just so she'd do it. *He really does love me*, she thought as she looked at her silver pinky ring, ashamed that her irritability had driven him away.

She eagerly held it up and out to Dr. Jillium, and the elegant woman took it, a smile quirking her lips as she eyed the notary's signature. "You went to a realtor's office?" she said in disbelief. "I was trying to get you into a bank."

Meg smirked knowingly. She hadn't been in a bank in five years. Between her fears and the internet, she'd turned avoiding people into an art form. "That's what Austin said, too." It had cost Austin fifty bucks whereas the bank notary would have done it for free, but he'd said it was worth every penny to get her to stop worrying about it. Slowly Meg's smile faded. That had been the day before he'd left. *I don't even remember what we argued about.*

Dr. Jillium's heels were silent on the carpet as she went behind her desk. Leaving the medical release there, she took the paper from the printer. "Then all you need to do is verify your statements concerning your side effects, or lack thereof, rather, and I can start you on a therapeutic dose."

"Thank you," Meg breathed in relief, and Dr. Jillium's focus sharpened, her grip not letting go of the paper when Meg tried to take it.

"There will be extra homework," she said as she released it, and Meg took the offered pen as well, her focus divided as she skimmed the document for accuracy before signing it.

"Bring it," Meg said as she handed the pen and paper back, willing to do anything to find some peace—some stillness.

Dr. Jillium took the paper with a slight smile. Narrow hips swaying, she returned to her desk and filed both papers before taking a key from her desk drawer and opening the smoke-glassed cabinet. Meg leaned to see a short row of amber pill vials, and then Dr. Jillium shifted to block her view.

"I need your assurance that you'll call me day or night if something doesn't feel right. I also want to know if any of the side effects we talked about begin to manifest. Hallucinations, both auditory and visual, extreme fear of strangers and avoidance of once relaxing activities are just a few of the problems that can occur in extreme cases, but they are always heralded by the minor ones. Seeing them won't necessarily mean taking you off Fitrecepon, but I want to know about it so we can adjust your levels. And then we have the diary."

"A diary?" Meg protested, having already gone around this with Dr. Jillium last year, and the year before that, and the year before that.

Dr. Jillium was smiling as she came back, a vial of pills and a student's theme book in her hands. "Fitrecepon is still highly experimental. I know your feelings about keeping a diary, but it's essential that I have an accurate account of your intake and emotions. You *will* keep a record of when you take it, and you *will* jot down at least a few sentences every day about how you feel. If you wait, whatever improvements you see will blur how you view the past and it won't be accurate. I'd very much like complete sentences and maybe a paragraph or two a day, but I know how painful that is for you."

Meg smirked at Dr. Jillium's dry sarcasm. Eyes rising up from the vial, she blurted, "I'll try."

Standing over her to look like a modern-day goddess, Dr. Jillium gave them to her. "I'd appreciate that."

The vial was the usual brown plastic, but to Meg, it felt priceless. The rattle of pills made it sound as if there weren't a lot in there, and setting the theme book aside, she read the instructions, seeing they were the same as for the trial dosage.

"One pill as needed for anxiety," Dr. Jillium said as Meg spun the vial to read it. "Do not take more than four a day, and wait at least four hours between doses. As before, you can take it on an empty stomach or full, but do make a note in your diary when you take it. I mean it, Meg."

Meg nodded at the woman's tight admonishment. She couldn't wait to get out of the office and try one. She might even be able to teach her class without jumping at every clink of a paintbrush. "I will," she said as she stood. She shoved the diary into her purse, but the pills went into her pocket. "Thank you, Dr. J."

"Wait up," Dr. Jillium admonished. "We haven't talked about your weekly goals."

Meg swung back around with a grimace. Dr. Jillium stood before the couch, her silhouette sharp against the cloudy sky outside.

"I want a firm commitment from you to increase your social interaction," the woman lectured. "Volunteer to teach a painting class at the retirement village. Go shopping at a new grocery store. And not at midnight, Meg. Make a new friend by next week. I want some real progress with Austin. Be prepared to talk next week about both yours and his needs and what you're looking for in a relationship. This is not a magic pill, and if you don't make an effort to lay down some new, positive patterns, I will take you off it. Understand?"

Meg felt breathless, but it was a good breathless, not the soul-stealing cramping of a nameless fear. "I do. Thanks, Dr. J." On impulse, she leaned across the narrow coffee table and gave her therapist a quick hug. Dropping back to her heels, she smiled sheepishly, thinking she'd crossed a line until Dr. Jillium reached out and squeezed her shoulder in understanding.

"Call me day or night if something seems wrong. Okay?" she prompted, and Meg nodded.

Perfunctory **Af**fection

"Promise," she said, then turned and showed herself out, clomping down the wood stairs and hustling over the vintage tile with only the faintest guilt for having dirtied them. She paused inside the building's tiny lobby, fumbling with the cap to her new meds until she could shake one of the light green tablets into her hand. She took it, holding it on her tongue while she found the bottled water she always carried, and with a hurried eagerness, washed it down.

"I'll write it down tonight," she whispered as she dropped the bottled water back in her purse next to the diary. Frumpy sweater coat over her arm, she strode out into the late morning. For the first time in weeks, it felt as if she might dare to believe there was hope left in her after all.

Three

The wide line of black narrowed as Meg eased the pressure of the brush on the canvas. The slick feel of the oil laying down whispered up through her arm, soothing, luring her into another stroke. Fingers nimble, she spun the second brush in her fingers into play and highlighted the previous brush stroke, lifting the pigment far too soon and leaving the length of the tree's branch unrealized.

The soft exhalation of understanding behind her was a shock and Meg stiffened, not liking having lost herself so deeply that she'd forgotten she wasn't alone. Back aching, she lifted her eyes from the high-contrast of black and white spilling onto the surface that hinted at a tortured tree at midnight. Her two-minute "technique demonstration" had stretched for an unexpected hour, right to the end of class. She'd found a place to hide from the anxiety, and she'd lost herself, oblivious that the entire class had clustered behind her to watch, not just the one student who'd asked. It hadn't been her intention to paint anything, but there it was, the twisted tree in stark black and white. *And I didn't know they were even there, crammed behind me like side-show gawkers.*

Not sure if it was the meds or pure concentration, she gripped her two brushes together, smearing the paint as she spun on a heel to face them. Her breath grew tight in her chest at their waiting expressions, and it was all she could do to not flee to the back of the room and out of the sun spilling in through the wide windows. The peaceful perfection in her mind was gone. *But I had it, if only for a moment.*

Meg took a steadying breath, hoping her students wouldn't see. "It's not so much using the actual pigment to define the space, but its absence," she said as she shifted behind the easel, dropping back an unexpected step when they clustered closer to try to pick apart the unique look. "Leave it unfinished," she said, glad they were focusing on the painting and not her. "It's the so-called imperfections that give it its strength and uniqueness. Allow the observer's mind to fill in the blanks to find the form, and the observer is empowered."

"I don't get it," a twenty-something woman complained, and the student next to her gave her a dry look. But it was obvious the class was over, and almost as one organism, they began to break up, the familiar clink of brushes spinning in cleaning jars and the scent of mineral spirits rising like a familiar balm.

The tightness in her chest eased as Meg crept back out from behind the canvas, studying them as they prepared to leave: seeing who put their brushes away still holding pigment with the intent to work at home, who cleaned them for the weekend, who looked at their own work with a frustrated determination.

An unexpected disappointment that the class was over colored her mood. Whether it had been the new meds or the pure bliss of painting, something had calmed her mind enough that she'd forgotten they were there, letting her find peace.

"Monday..." she began, voice breaking. She'd shown them something unique, and a few were beginning to look past her frumpy clothes and take her seriously instead of as an artistic fluke. "Monday," she said again, and several students paused to attentively listen. "I want to see from you three examples of the same object, same perspective. Choose something simple enough to get three full renderings, but complex enough that you get a feel for the exercise. Make the first the way you usually would, the second pull out half the dark, the third, pull out half the light. See what you can come up with. And have fun with it."

Her pulse was fast, but she forced herself to maintain eye contact and that startled-deer smile she knew she was wearing. *I'm the flakey artist in residence*, she thought. *Quirky, not scared.*

"Three renderings?" that same young woman complained. "Just because *she* doesn't have anything to do over the weekend doesn't mean I don't."

"Shut up, Lisa," her friend muttered as she carefully wrapped her brushes in clear plastic so she wouldn't have to clean them. "I know three people who will take your slot if you want to quit."

Meg's flush of gratitude hung with her, but she still felt awkward as she waited for the last of her students to leave before venturing out past her canvas. Slowly her shoulders eased, and she exhaled in relief. *One down, an entire semester to go*, she thought. But it had been a good three hours. A positive pattern, as Dr. J would have said.

Only now did Meg take a critical look of what was supposed to have been a quick, demonstrative sketch of an old oak tree hung with wisteria. Nodding, she decided it was good enough to keep working on. Austin was gone, and she'd need something to do this weekend. If she was lucky, the unusual sensation of three solid hours with no anxiety would come home with it.

"Sure feels like a magic pill to me," Meg said, her voice filling the empty room as she went to clean her tools. The stark white and heavy black on the twin brushes had been smeared to a muted gray of commonality in her careless-ness. She'd have to start over.

Quick from long practice, she scraped off the excess color on her tiny three-color thumb palette. Her brushes were next, and she watched the flash of bright and dull mix into nothing in the bath of mineral spirits. Seeing every-thing fade to a dull gray, it was easy to see what creatively pulled her. It was the extremes: the light, the dark. The spreading middle ground was lost in the noise much as average people were never noticed as they moved through existence. *Like me.*

Her brushes clattered to the counter, and Meg used the pigment-stained tub of lotion to rehydrate her hands when the oil-stripping mineral spirits bled through the drying cloths. She gave her bare nails a wan smile. She'd never have polish, but the bare nails went with the homespun artist look she had going for her. Sighing, she wondered if maybe with this new medication, she could actually get to the mall while the sun was up. *Dr. J would be pleased.*

Going back to her canvas, she tucked everything in her large satchel purse, pulled the canvas carefully from the easel, gazed over the quiet, sun-drenched space, and left leaving the door unlocked behind her. Maybe the last few hours weren't just a skip in the beat of her daily hell, but a new beginning of peace.

Kim Harrison

The thought brought her head up, and Meg felt good enough to acknowledge the few people she met on her way out of the fine arts building. Emboldened, she let her free arm swing, enjoying the warm spring sun as she went down the wide steps to the quad's sidewalk.

But a questioning admonishment that she had no right to feel this happy sent her eyes to the campus clock tower. She couldn't take another pill for hours, and a nervous tension flashed through her. It left behind the insistent feeling that she'd been remiss about something.

I should call Austin, she thought as she angled toward the quad's central fountain. It was a beautiful day, and there wouldn't be anyone going to the movies. With the stress of her last class behind her, she felt as if she could handle someone sitting behind her in the dark. But even as she thought it, she wondered if it was a sign of improvement, or just finding a better way to avoid her triggers.

Meg's grip on her canvas tightened in annoyance. The chill shadow of the fountain's statue fell upon her, and she looked up, shifting until the sun was behind the cold gray stone. The lithe, graceful form of an angel was forever pouring out one of the jars at her feet, but what caught Meg's attention were the glistening strands of spider silk floating from the goddess's head, catching the sun and glowing like glory itself.

Spiders, Meg realized. Hundreds, if not thousands, of young spiders were ballooning away to new territories.

Perfunctory
Af**fection**

Setting her canvas down, Meg rummaged in her bag for her phone. If she could get a good enough shot, she'd use it as a subject for her students. The stark contrast of sky and golden thread, of cold stone and warm sun, was amazing.

"Got it," Meg breathed, and then after seeing what she'd captured, she took a few more from the same angle.

It wasn't until she was putting her phone away that she noticed the petite woman standing just outside the fountain's mist zone, a slip of tissue-thin paper in her hand, a puzzled frown on her angular face. She was dressed impeccably in a red skirt, white leggings, and a matching white blouse. A red leather coat and stylish beret warded off the lingering chill of the morning rain. Sunglasses hid her eyes and made her blond hair seem even brighter, but the trendy red frames made her seem as if she belonged on the colorful west coast, not here in the dour, conventional east.

Student? Meg thought upon seeing the class list in her hand. She was certainly flamboyant enough for one, but the quality of her clothes were outside most students reach. She was slightly shorter than Meg, well-proportioned, slim, blond, in her late twenties, pretty under makeup so carefully applied that it looked natural...and clearly lost.

"Excuse me," the woman called to a student passing on a hoverboard that didn't live up to its name. "Do you know where the language arts building is? Hello?" she added sarcastically, her high voice holding an unfamiliar accent when the kid kept going, ignoring her.

"Not today, huh?" Slim hand on a narrow hip, she watched him vanish down the tree-lined sidewalk. "Why are all the cute ones taken or blind?"

Meg's hands went clammy, and she screwed up her courage. Dr. Jillium expected her to come back with news of having made a friend by next week, and after three hours of relatively anxiety-free class, she'd do anything to not lose access to her new meds. But it was more than that as Meg picked her canvas up and forced herself to the sunny side of the fountain. She wanted real improvement, not simply finding new ways to avoid what made her anxious.

"You, ah, need some help finding your class?" she said, feeling awkward.

The young woman spun. Perfect lips parted in surprise, she looked Meg up and down over her red-rimmed glasses, her gaze lingering on Meg's necklace, then widening in disbelief at the ankle-length skirt and the long sweater coat.

Meg's chin lifted at what she thought was disappointment in the back of the young woman's eyes, and she waited for the lordly assurance that she "didn't need any help, thanks." If the woman wanted to stand in the middle of the quad and accost the male student body under the excuse of needing help, it wasn't Meg's problem.

But then the woman's eyes dropped to the canvas, and Meg would have sworn she heard her gasp. "Yes. Yes I do," she said, her voice fast as she closed the distance between them. Her smile had become real and welcoming, and her tone almost a coaxing persuasion that Meg had never heard directed at her before. "Language arts building?" she added, flashing a brilliant, white-toothed smile. "I've got a class later and I want to check out the facilities. My faculty welcome packet didn't include a map of the campus."

Teacher, Meg thought, clamping down on the familiar rise of a nameless fear. Her eyes darted to the campus clock, the need to take a pill growing. But she wasn't going to pop pills in front of this blond goddess who needed her help, and she stilled her jittering foot, telling herself it was her imagination, her mind telling her there's danger when there wasn't any. *Dr. J wants me to make a new friend, not a pen pal.* "You're staff?" Meg said, forcing a smile. "Me too." Eyes rolling, she gestured to her dowdy, tree-hugger outfit to try to explain her lack of polish. "In case you can't tell," she finished dryly.

But the woman didn't seem to care anymore, leaning to try to see the canvas. "Is that your work?" she said, staring. "It is absolutely gorgeous." She took her glasses off, her blue eyes flicking up first to Meg's artist-themed necklace, then back down to the painting. "Can I see?"

Pride made it easy to ignore her anxiety as she swung her canvas up, the strong sun making the image almost glow.

Kim Harrison

The water from the fountain chattered, and Meg had a brief thought to move farther away from the spray—until the woman beside her touched the canvas almost reverently. "A painter," she almost seemed to breathe. "This is amazing work. I've never seen anything like it. I don't know what it is. It's not minimalist. I'd call it...intuitive, maybe. You've left out parts not to define areas as much as to invite the eye to complete them. Oh, this is outstanding." Putting her glasses back on, she studied the canvas again. "I bet your classes are overflowing."

Not used to the praise, Meg flushed. "Do you paint?" she asked, and the woman looked at her from over her glasses.

"Me? No." Letting go of the canvas, she dropped back a step, smiling as if they were old friends. "But I know unique when I see it. I'm a linguist. I'm a guest teacher this semester while some old fart is on sabbatical, and then I'll be moving on to the next job."

"Oh." Meg couldn't ask for a better friend, one that would satisfy Dr. Jillium, give Meg practice in laying down "positive patterns," and yet not hang around to the inevitable fall-apart stage. Pulse fast, she let her painting drop to hang at her side, and the woman finally took her eyes off it.

"I'm Haley," she said, extending her slim hand.

"Meg. I teach alternative oil techniques." Haley's nails were exquisitely painted, and Meg felt shabby as she took her hand and gave it a shake. The woman's grip was cool and light, and almost as soon as they touched, Haley jerked away.

Surprised at the fast motion, Meg froze. "Don't move," Haley said, her melodious voice serious as she eyed Meg's shoulder. "It's a spider."

"Oh, God. Get it off," Meg demanded, her eyes wide as Haley brushed her shoulder and stomped on the pavers.

"I hate spiders," Haley said, actually shuddering, but she *had* gotten it off her and killed it, and Meg thought anyone who could do that for a complete stranger was worth getting to know.

"The wind must have shifted." Meg turned to the fountain, but either the spiders were gone or the silk couldn't be seen from this angle, and the angel poured her unending vial into the fountain unadorned.

"Wind?" Haley questioned, and Meg set down her canvas to find her phone.

"They were ballooning off the fountain. See? I'm going to make my students paint it on Monday."

Haley cautiously leaned forward and looked. "Oh. So they were."

Feeling as if she'd done something wrong, Meg closed her phone out and dropped it in her pocket with her meds. *She doesn't like spiders. Why are you showing her a picture of thousands of them, doofus?* "The language arts building is across campus where the old dramatic arts used to be,"

Meg said, pointing. "I'm heading home and it's on the way. I can walk you there."

Meg winced, thinking she sounded needy even to herself, but Haley was smiling again from behind her dark glasses.

"Would you?" Haley gushed, and Meg picked her canvas up as Haley went to get a large satchel resting in the shadow of the fountain. "Thank you so much. I'm awful with directions. And I'm usually not this clueless, but I was called in with only a week's notice. I don't even have a real apartment yet. I hate living out of a suitcase. I don't even know where the good restaurants are. And to top it off my alarm was set for the wrong time zone and I overslept." She readjusted the large bag on her shoulder. "That way?" she prompted, and Meg mentally shook herself.

"Yes." It felt more than odd as Meg took the lead. That this amazingly polished woman didn't seem to mind that they looked like opposite ends of the cool meter seemed too good to be true, and Meg couldn't help but notice that Haley met every person's eye as if proud to be walking beside her.

Haley was everything Meg wasn't: bubbly, outgoing, dressed for success with her gold jewelry flashing in the sun and her dark glasses this year's style. Her steps matched Meg's exactly as if they were long-time friends, and her heels clicked smartly on the sidewalk to pull attention to them both. Her makeup made her face seem to glow when she looked up at the passing oaks and asked if Meg knew how long they had been growing. Even the woman's hair was fabulous as it lifted in the slight breeze, like spun gold even in the shade, nothing like Meg's annoying curls that couldn't even be brushed lest they poof out.

Haley was the popular girl grown up into success, and Meg slowed their fast pace as she found herself reluctant to find the sidewalk's crossroads where they'd have to part, Haley to her class and Meg to her dark apartment.

"So you're a guest teacher?" Meg asked when Haley's ongoing prattle cut off with a sudden yawn. "Where have you taught?"

Haley flushed as if realizing she'd been monopolizing the conversation. "Everywhere," she said, her attention coming up from the painting. "I like to travel, and my boyfriend's job can be done anywhere, so we get around. Neither of us want kids, so we have no reason to settle." Eyes in the oak branches, she played with her gold necklace. It held a string of birds, all clustered together like pearls, and it clinked pleasantly.

"How nice," Meg said, but inside, she was putting herself in the geek spot. Why was this woman even talking to her? Of course she'd have a boyfriend, and how amazingly lucky he had a job that could move as easily as her.

"We spent an entire year in San Francisco," Haley said, arms swinging freely. "Before that, it was New Orleans. Before that, outside of New York." She shuddered, her eyes lost behind those dark glasses. "New York was hard," she admitted. "You'd think it would be easier with so many people about, but no one sees you in a big city. I'm originally from a tiny place up north called Perfection."

Meg bobbed her head, thinking it must be hard for the popular girl to suddenly be a small fish in a very large pond. Their parting point was just up ahead, and Meg's pace slowed even more. "Didn't the university give you a list of apartments?"

"They did." Haley didn't seem to notice their slower pace, her face turned to the oaks again. "But I don't want to get a car if we don't have to, and I'd like to be near the good restaurants. I don't cook much, and what Rorry does can't be called cooking." Her smile grew stiff in an unshared memory. "I bet you know where to eat."

The sudden urge to tell Haley about her apartment building vanished. Though within walking distance of the campus, it wasn't near any restaurants. But the real reason she kept silent was because she was sure her idea of a good meal wasn't the same as Haley's.

"I know a few nice spots," she hedged, surprised that though she felt odd walking beside Haley, there wasn't a whisper of angst. At all. Even the passing students who noticed them seemed harmless. *I should stop wearing such frumpy clothes*, she thought as she smiled at the student and his service dog at the edge of the sidewalk.

Perfunctory **Af**fection

"Oh, God, slide over," Haley whispered, grabbing Meg's arm and bodily shifting her to the far side of the sidewalk.

"He won't run into us," Meg said, and Haley shook her head, her grip easing as the dog and his master moved past.

"I'm deathly allergic," she said, head down to find a wadded-up, creased tissue in her satchel.

But they had reached the crossroad, and Meg scuffed to a halt, her sneakers looking odd against Haley's bright red heels as the woman pretended to blow her nose. "That's your building there," Meg said, pointing, and Haley stared blankly at her for a moment before turning to it, her expression brightening. "I'm going that way," Meg added, looking the other direction. Desperately hoping that Haley didn't think she was brushing her off, and she added, "You should talk to campus services. They can at least give you a listing of who's got available rooms."

Her expression pinched with gratitude, Haley took Meg's hand. "Thanks so much, Meg," she gushed. "It was wonderful to meet you and you were so nice to help me." Fingers slipping away, she glanced at the canvas between them. "If you're not doing anything tonight, do you want to get together for dinner? You could show Rorry and me the town, and I wouldn't have to eat whatever he tries to cook."

"Tonight?" A surge of panic washed through Meg, and her hand slapped her pocket where the pills lay. She wanted to take one now so she'd have the courage to say yes.

"We could make it a double date," Haley said brightly, looking like a goddess in the dappled sun making it through the oak leaves. "Bring your boyfriend and we'll meet at the fountain. I know how to find that!" she said with a laugh. "Around seven thirty, maybe? I've got class until seven."

Meg blinked in consternation. A double date? She'd have to ask Austin. What if he said no?

Misunderstanding, Haley's expression fell. "You've got plans," she said, somehow sounding vulnerable. "It's Friday. I shouldn't have imposed. I just wanted to thank you for being so nice."

"No, I don't have any plans," Meg blurted. *I don't need a pill to say yes.* "Seven thirty would be okay, sure." Her free hand crept up and clutched her necklace to hide her hurting chest. The anxiety wasn't as bad, but it was back, and Meg could almost cry, afraid that Haley would think she didn't like her if she said no. She'd have to call Austin and work things out. But a double date would knock out two of Dr. Jillium's goals in one trying evening. Just a few hours to work through, and then she could relax the rest of the week. *I can do this.* "I need to ask Austin, though," she mumbled, and Haley seemed to bounce right back, her smile in place as she tucked her hair behind an ear.

"Fabulous!" Haley hoisted her satchel higher up her shoulder. "We'll meet you and Austin at the fountain. You're going to love Rorry. Everyone loves Rorry." Still smiling, she gave Meg a wave and turned away. Meg could have sworn that her gaze left her canvas last. "Wish me luck finding my room!" she called over her shoulder, steps fast as she strode to the language arts building.

"Luck!" Meg called back, but she didn't think perfect Haley from Perfection needed any such thing.

Chest tight, Meg turned away. Still standing in the middle of the sidewalk, she fumbled in a near panic to open the vial of pills that Dr. Jillium gave her. Her hands shook as she sifted one into her palm, and breath held, she swallowed it dry.

The snap of the cap going back on was loud, and only now did Meg look up to see if anyone had noticed. But the quad was nearly empty, and Meg dropped the bottle back into her pocket, anxiously waiting for the meds to kick in.

She had said yes. Now all she had to do was convince Austin to come with her and get through the night.

"I can do this," she said as she headed across campus to her apartment. "I can live without being afraid."

Four

Phone in hand, Meg stood at the living room window and looked down at the apartment's parking lot, watching her downstairs neighbor struggle with too many bags of groceries. Frustration had furrowed her brow, frustration in that she couldn't decide if she should call Austin back or just forget the whole thing. He hadn't responded to her text this afternoon about wanting to talk to him, and it was getting late. Knowing Austin, he might just show up after work, but the parking spot that the two-room, second-floor apartment had come with was empty, and she nervously spun the ring that Austin had given her around her pinky finger.

The growing likelihood that she might have to go alone and explain why Austin was a no-show left her cold, but the thought of standing Haley up was horrifying. The woman would probably think she was a spaz and never speak to her again. That she had even spoken to her once seemed a miracle.

"Why did I ever say yes to this?" she said, almost oblivious to the TV talking quietly to itself. She didn't have much to wear that wouldn't look frumpy beside Haley's perfection. Worse, she had no clue where to take them. What if she got there and had a panic attack before the bread even came?

A quick movement at the edge of the cars caught her attention, and Meg stiffened when a scruffy dog raced across the parking lot and was gone. It was the same one that had been with that homeless guy who'd yelled at her outside of Dr. Jillium's, and she frowned. The thought to call the pound came and went; the dog had an owner, even if that owner had no home himself.

The sudden sharp knock at the door shocked through Meg, and she jumped, glancing at her phone for the time before tossing it into her purse and crossing the dimly lit living room. It wouldn't be Austin. True, he had left, but his things were still here and he'd just walk in.

"Yes?" she said loudly as she tweaked the blah-brown curtains beside the door and looked out at the swarthy man in a simple, dark suit.

"Meg Seton?" the man said, his teeth looking very white against his dark complexion as he smiled. He was holding up a badge, and Meg blanched as she saw he was from the FBI. *Oh, God, what did I do?*

"Yes. What do you want?" she asked, shrinking away from the window.

"I'm Daniel Hun. I work for the FBI." The man held his badge right up to the window for a moment before tucking the wallet away and taking out a small tablet. "I'm trying to find this man. Goes by the name of Christopher. Have you seen him?"

Meg leaned closer to the window, calmer now that she knew he wasn't there for her. Not that she'd done anything to warrant the FBI's attention. The tablet showed a young-ish man in his early thirties, clean shaven, his blond hair cut evenly about his ears. He was in a set of scrubs, but the rummy look in his blue eyes said patient, not doctor.

"We suspect he may be in this area," Daniel said, jerking Meg's attention back.

"Hang on a sec." Feeling braver, Meg let the curtain fall and opened the door. She stood in the threshold, to take the offered tablet to get a closer look. It almost looked like the homeless guy. "Maybe," she said, squinting to give him a scruffy beard and matted hair. "But he was a mess," she added. "Why do you want him? Is he dangerous?"

Daniel smiled as he took the tablet back. "I'd say he was… erratic, not dangerous. I need to get him back to the hospital."

Nodding, Meg dropped back a step. "I saw a homeless man that looked like him."

"Homeless?" Daniel ran a hand through his dark, lightly curling hair as he rocked back on one heel to look behind him at the parking lot. It was beginning to get dark, and the need to get ready to go made Meg fidget.

"With a little dog," she added. Her hand was on the door, but Daniel pushed forward, his eyes alight.

"That sounds likely," he said, a faint, unfamiliar accent beginning to show as he got excited. "Where did you see him?"

He was too close, and Meg took a step back. "The other end of the quad, near the old textile building. Look, I've got to go. I'm sorry I can't help you."

"No, you've been very helpful. Thank you." Daniel retreated to the railing, his smile never dimming. "Let me know if you see him again, will you please?"

Meg hesitated, then took the card he was extending. She'd seen that dog not three seconds before Daniel had knocked on her door. But he hadn't asked about a dog, only the man. "Are you sure he's not dangerous?"

"I can't say anything for certain, ma'am." Daniel was looking at the parking lot, his thoughts clearly on Christopher. "There's a reason he's in the hospital." His attention came back to Meg, and he tapped his head as if to say he was crazy.

"Oh."

"Call me if you see him again," Daniel said as he walked backward to the open-aired stairway down to the ground level. "The longer he stays off his medications, the more erratic he will be."

"Yes sir. Thank you." Meg shut the door, wondering why she thanked him. "I am such a doofus," she whispered. She should have told him about the dog instead of sending him halfway across campus, but something didn't sound right. How had he known her name if he was doing a casual door-to-door, and why would he tell her the man he was looking for was a mental-hospital runaway? That he was potentially dangerous? Daniel hadn't owed her any explanation, and he'd given her one.

"Six thirty already?" she whispered as she went to the window to watch Daniel walk away, his arm swinging eagerly and his pace fast as he talked to someone on his phone. *No car?* she mused silently as she sat on the arm of the couch, arms crossed over her middle.

Daniel's card was still in her hand, and after a moment's consideration, she dropped it into her purse. Her phone made a silent statement, and her worry that Austin hadn't called her back returned. She'd only said she'd wanted to talk to him, not knowing how he'd react to the idea of a double date when their last conversation had gone down bad.

Frustrated, she stared at the TV, tuned to Austin's favorite show of a professional couple redesigning someone else's living space. It was the big reveal, and the screen alternated between the dingy, cluttered, disjointed *before* to the open, clean, uncluttered *after*. Everything was perfect, the designers idea of what should exist.

Mood sour, Meg sent her gaze to her own apartment, dark with its mostly northern exposure and tiny windows set to look out over the parking lot. Everything was brown: Austin's lumpy brown couch, worn brown carpet she hated, raggedy brown drapes that came with the place, flat, brown walls that still had holes in them from the previous tenants. Even the tile and cupboards in the open kitchen behind her were brown, glinting dully in an overhead light half as bright as it should be.

Her paintings were the only thing in the entire apartment that stood out, the small canvases scattered over the space to bring in spots of color. The one of the clock tower in the spring was a vivid blue and black. Her favorite was of the nearby lake on a hot July day, all green and white; she could almost hear the cicadas. Her latest of a imaginary tree was set on her work easel in an artificially bright spotlight to mimic the sun. Over the TV was the first painting she'd done after her mother had died: a self-portrait whose disjointed lines made an uneasy expression. It never failed to amaze Meg how little there needed to be of a face for the mind to complete the picture, and it had been the first hint of her new style that had gotten her a job, and perhaps a place in the art history books.

Suddenly she realized that though she and Austin had been sharing the apartment for almost three years, her canvases were the only things that said she existed.

Perfunctory
Af**fection**

Austin's magazines were still where he had left them, and his gaming console waited at his favorite chair. His shoes were tucked under the couch, and the lamp he made in high school shop cast a paltry glow over the dull banality of her existence. Her heart ached at Austin's coat hanging beside hers at the door, his heavy winter shoes next to her boots, abandoned when she'd began wearing sneakers this spring.

Her eyes flicked back to the TV, and she grimaced at the homeowner crying in joy over the transformation. Meg's existence was a depressing comparison to the bright openness on the TV. But then Meg smirked when she noticed that for all its light and airy design, the redesigned living room didn't have a TV. Two days after the designers left, the homeowners would probably stick one in their new reading nook or in place of that specially designed picture on the wall. Two weeks, and all the things that the TV crew had taken out to declutter would be back: the family photos, the bar-themed coasters, the old chair that was comfortable but shabby, the foot massager and tattered couch throw for the dog that didn't fit with the designers color scheme—all fighting for space with the new art-deco balls and scented candles.

"You can't live in perfection," she whispered. "We are a cluttered mess." With a snap, she turned off the TV. She stood, her chest tightening as she looked at Austin's things scattered over the apartment as a painful reminder. If she didn't go out, she'd be sitting in this brown room eating mac and cheese and watching home improvement shows on a Friday night.

In a surge of self-preservation, Meg vowed that wouldn't happen. "I will make positive patterns," she said, arms swinging as she strode into the bedroom and into the huge walk-in closet. "And I don't need Austin to do it." *God help me, more brown*, she thought, blanching as the overhead light flickered on and held steady. "I'm not going to stand Haley up, even if I do look like a tree hugger next to her," she muttered as she pushed past her usual outfits to where her gallery event clothes hung. "Even if I have to leave in the middle of dinner, I am going to try."

From the living room, her phone tinkled an incoming call. Meg froze, then ran to get it, having to shuffle past the empty diary Dr. Jillium had given her to find it. It was Austin, and fingers fumbling, she hit accept. *Six thirty-five. It's not too late. He might be able to make it if he is on campus.*

"Austin, you got my message?" she said breathlessly, their past argument making her sound needy even to herself.

"I did," he said, his ever-present acceptance and patience easing tightness in her chest. "But I was going to call you tonight, anyway. I wanted to find out how your class went today. I called admissions. Fifteen students! Way to go, Meg. I'm impressed."

"Thanks. Class was great," she said, her gaze going to her tree, and he grunted in a pleased surprise. "I started a new canvas."

"That's wonderful. What is it?"

"A wisteria-draped tree." Phone to her ear, she headed back to her closet. "I'm using my new technique. It's not as effective on an organic form as one the human brain is wired to fill in the blanks with, but I brought in a little of my watercolor techniques, and it worked. I really like it." *I have nothing to wear.*

"I can't wait to see it," he said, and she fumbled for her next words. There was so much more that she wanted to say than invite him on a double date.

"Dr. J says I need to talk to you," she said as she flipped past a blue jumpsuit. *Good God, why is that even in here?* "And I want to," she added, hearing how that sounded. "Not just because she says I should. Damn it, this is coming out wrong." Head bowed over the phone, she touched his sweater hanging beside hers. "I miss you."

"I miss you, too," he said softly, but the expected, "I want to move back in," didn't follow, and as she pushed aside her cardigans as being too frumpy, Meg wondered how long they could both live in this limbo. Austin had been more than good for her, helping her through her panic attacks until they were daily instead of unending, and encouraging her without letting her lie to herself that avoidance was actually progress. She owed him a lot, and that he'd left to give her space to find herself hurt.

And in a flash of insight, she realized that was why he'd left. She wouldn't make any real progress if he stayed, a helpful, loving crutch, so he had left, leaving enough of himself that she wouldn't feel as if he'd abandoned her forever. *And I yelled at him for leaving*, she thought, warming in embarrassment.

"Dr. J started me on a therapeutic level of that new med," she said, rushing to fill the silence. "I was able to teach an entire class before I got antsy." Antsy was her code name for panic attack, and Austin made a knowing, encouraging sound. "I, ah, met a new teacher this afternoon, and she wants to go out on a double date."

"Really! Meg, that's great," Austin said brightly, and Meg cringed, feeling as if she was being pushy.

"Tonight..." she said hesitantly. "If you're not busy. And you want to."

"I'm not busy, no," he said quickly, and Meg breathed easier, glad his purposeful abandonment didn't include this. "It's kind of short notice, but I'm the last person to say no to spontaneity."

Thank God, she thought in relief as she flicked through her skirts, all of them too long or of a heavy wool. *Frumpy, frumpy, and more frumpy.* "Thank you so much, Austin," she said, deciding on a pair of dark blue jeans she'd only worn once and which still looked new. "Her name is Haley. Haley

and Rorry. She's a guest teacher for the semester." *A black
sweater. Not the long one, but the short-sleeved one.* "They want
us to show them the town."

"Meg…" Austin said warily, and she warmed, the memory of having left him holding the bag on their last double
date filling her.

"It's just dinner," she said. "I promise I won't leave if I
have a panic attack. I'll just go sit in the bathroom."

"For twenty minutes?" he said, and then he sighed. "I
just don't want to get out somewhere and then have you
want to leave."

Meg frowned. Suddenly the sweater looked too dull, and
she fingered a light brown one. It was almost gold, really. "If
you don't want to come, that's okay," she said defensively.
Maybe she was wrong on why he'd left.

"That's not what I'm saying," Austin asserted. "I want
to go. You know I want to support you in you making new
patterns, but I also know your track record and I don't want
you to try to do too much and end up in your room again
for a week."

The sweater wasn't gold, it was brown, and she hung it
back up. "I haven't done that in over a year," she said coldly.

"Sorry," Austin said, and she could almost see his eyes
crinkled in dismay. "Look, I don't want to argue. You know
I'd do anything for you. I want to meet your new friends.
What time should I pick you up?"

A surge of excitement washed through her, and her fingers reaching for that black sweater curled under. Still didn't know what she was going to wear or where to take them, but she was adamant that Haley not see their old-lady car. It had belonged to her mother, the maroon, late model Volvo still serviceable even after Meg had run it into a tree three years ago. Austin was the only one who drove it, but the dented front had never been fixed, and she was embarrassed.

Anxiety pinched her brow, and Meg touched her pocket to be sure she had her pills. "We were going to meet at the fountain and go to one of the restaurants within walking distance," she said, planning on blaming the restaurant's lack of quality on their limited range. "Haley doesn't have a car, and she wants to get to know the campus."

"What time?" Austin asked patiently.

Meg fingered a yellow sweater. Her mother had given it to her, and she'd never worn it, thinking the gold thread highlights were too flashy. Next to Haley, they'd probably never be noticed. "Can you be ready by seven thirty?"

"Shaved and dressed?" Austin echoed, and Meg warmed again. "Sure. I'll come over and walk you to the fountain. It's easier to park in our slot and walk than find a place in the student parking."

"Thank you, Austin. You're the best." He was going to come with her. Relieved, Meg decided the yellow sweater was too much. She'd wear her interview slacks with the black sweater. That meant heels, and with a wash of worry, she decided that wouldn't work either. Haley might think she was trying to impress her, even if she was.

"Don't thank me, Meg. You know I'd do anything for you. I'm glad you feel ready for a night out."

"Love you," she whispered, breath held as she waited.

"I love you, too. See you in ten."

He hung up, and before Meg could end the call, the tight walls of the closet seemed to close in on her. Her pulse raced, and her chest hurt. She was going out on a double date, and it was going to be a disaster.

"No, damn it, no!" she whispered as her hands began to shake. It was the beginnings of a full-blown panic attack. Eyes wide, Meg pushed back into the clothes, surrounding herself with the warm fabrics and the scent of Austin still lingering among his shirts. Breath fast, she fumbled for the bottle of pills in her pocket, frantic as she shook one out and swallowed it dry.

"Not this time. Not this time..." she whispered. "Please, not this time." Eyes closed, she leaned against the wall and waited for her pulse to slow. Slowly her calm returned. Pushing back up and out through Austin's cotton shirts, Meg took a slow breath.

The yellow sweater would be fine, she decided as she reached for it, her hands once again steady. Her sneakers

Kim Harrison

wouldn't look odd with the jeans, and she'd make sure they didn't go anywhere they would look out of place.

Taking everything in hand, Meg left her closet, wondering if she had time to put on a little makeup. She wasn't going to ruin this chance. She'd make this work.

Five

M eg had always thought that the chatter of the quad's fountain was louder at night. The hiss and bubble of the angel forever pouring her vial into the pool among the waterfalls and spray was peaceful and serene when the campus grew quiet, the shadow and light created by underwater and overhead lights giving an unexpected softness to the woman's face. Her smile became beatific, and the folds of her garment seemed supple enough to move in the breeze.

Sitting on the dry edge of the fountain, Meg craned her neck to see the angel's face, recalling the spiders ballooning off her head this afternoon. Most were gone now, but several had stayed as evidenced by new, tiny webs among the folds of stone, billowing in the air currents created by the rushing water. On the far side of the fountain, a young couple laughed as they threw coins and wished for high marks in their chemistry class. The rhythmic thumping of running shoes came and went with the jingling of a collar as a jogger and his dog rushed past. In the near distance, a guy in plaid ran for a building, a ruler falling from his stack of books, unnoticed in his headlong dash to make his class.

"I love the beginning of the semester," Austin said from beside her, and Meg's smile widened. He had an unexpected polish tonight, looking good in the casual jacket, slacks, and clean shirt he'd taken from their closet. He'd shaved at their apartment, too, and hearing him getting ready had filled her with a surprising sense of peace: the small sounds of the water, the clink of the razor, the moist warmth of the bathroom holding the scent of his aftershave. She missed him, even if it had been only a few days.

Austin checked his phone for the time, his hand looking awkward and wrong as he held it. Some of the tendons had never healed properly, but that wasn't why Meg warmed. Haley was late.

"There were spiders ballooning off the statue this afternoon," Meg said to distract him, and Austin turned, his thin eyebrows high.

"Really?"

Nodding, Meg leaned to get her phone out of her purse currently sitting on the pavers at her feet. "I'm going to use it as a painting prompt on Monday," she said as she swiped through her photos and showed him. "Maybe pull everyone outside and do an onsite demonstration."

Austin's smile widened. "Fifteen easels at the fountain will certainly increase the campus awareness of your class."

Meg's smile faded. "Then again, maybe not." She closed her phone down, guilt rising as she saw her diary still in her purse. She'd write something tonight after their date.

Sighing, Austin crossed his arms over his chest and leaned deeper into the cold stone, his bad leg stretched out to ease the tension in it. "You're sure she said the fountain?"

Nodding, Meg's gaze went deep into the darkening quad, looking for Haley's bright presence. Maybe it was all a bad joke and Haley was in one of the surrounding buildings, laughing at her and taking bets with the other beautiful people as to how long she would wait.

"You should call her," Austin suggested, and Meg winced.

"I, ah, don't have her number."

Smile never fading, Austin reached for his phone. "What's her last name? I'll look her up in the campus directory."

Cringing, Meg muttered, "I never asked."

Expression blanking, Austin's reach faltered. "You didn't ask? Meg…"

Kim Harrison

"I'm not that good at this, okay?" she snapped, angry at herself. "I didn't know there was a protocol to making new friends."

"That's not what I'm saying." Austin put an arm around her, tugging her sideways into him with a gentle admonishment, but it made Meg feel even more stupid.

"Then what are you saying?" she mumbled, eyes down as his warmth eased against her.

"That it would be easier to get in touch with her if you had her last name or phone number," he said with a dry humor, and she met his gaze.

"You think?"

Austin gave her another squeeze before turning his head back down over his phone and his news feed. Meg's brief flush of contentment faltered. The sound of the water seemed to fade behind the squeak of a food cart, the scent of popcorn reaching them long before the man pushing it would. Frustrated, Meg took a breath to come up with an excuse for Haley's tardiness, then hesitated. There was a dog looking at her from under a nearby bench. It was that same scruffy mutt, and Meg's brow furrowed. "I had a guy from the FBI banging on our door this afternoon," she said, and Austin looked up from his phone.

"You're kidding. What did he want?"

"He was looking for the guy who owns that dog," she said, and Austin followed her gaze to the bench. But the bench was empty. "Wow, he was just there," she said, and Austin sighed as he put his phone away.

"Maybe the popcorn cart scared him off," he said, then added softly, "I don't think they're going to show." Anxiety was a hot dart through her, but Austin seemed happy; all but one of his fingers curled under to touch his palm as he gently arranged her hair and smiled fondly at her. "I almost hope they don't," he added. "You want some popcorn?"

"Why not," she said glumly as she stood and pushed off the fountain's wall. They hadn't even discussed where to take Haley and Rorry yet. Well, they had, but they'd not come to any decisions. Just as well. It looked as if she wasn't coming.

"Oh, don't be like that," Austin said with a playful sourness. "We can walk around the quad, eat popcorn, and see what the freshmen are drinking this year. You know, like we used to do."

"Sounds good. No, I'll get it," she said as she caught the eye of the vendor and motioned for two bags. Eyebrows high, Austin hesitated in his reach for his wallet and settled back even as the vendor angled toward them. She couldn't bear seeing Austin's hand twisted up when he counted out change.

"No extra butter. Thanks," she said, fighting a not-unexpected nervousness as the vendor scooped two bags of steaming popcorn. As disappointed as she was that Haley was a no-show, a sense of relief was filling her. She should have known someone as perfect as Haley would find something better to do on a Friday night, and someone more exciting to do it with.

Austin waited on the fountain's wall, his legs stretched out as Meg shuffled through her purse to find a fiver. "If she shows, she can have my popcorn," he said as she paid the man and took the two bags.

"You don't think she's going to show," she said as the vendor shoved the bill in his pocket and pushed his cart into motion, headed for the freshman mixer just now starting on the far end of the quad.

Austin shrugged as she handed him one of the warm bags and, she sat beside him, her eyes on the darkening quad. The scent of hot butter bathed her face to remind her of how she and Austin had met. "You said seven thirty." Head tilted back, Austin dropped a handful of popcorn into his mouth. "It's almost eight. By campus standards, the class has been canceled."

Grimacing, Meg watched the vendor vanish into the darkness following the sound of laughter and a steady beat. "I'm willing to float her a few more minutes." But the popcorn smelled wonderful, and she took a wad, deciding it was as good a dinner as anything. The salt and butter woke up her appetite, and she sat back against the cold stone, depressed.

Perfunctory Af**fection**

Haley had stood her up. But at least Austin was here, reminding her that this one sucky person did not mean she was friendless. Mood sour, she ate another kernel. "Thanks for coming out here with me," she said softly. "I miss you." She swallowed hard, feeling exposed as she added, "Why don't you move back in?"

"I will." His head was down over his popcorn. "Soon, I hope. Dr. Jillium thinks I've become a crutch. That I'm keeping you from moving forward."

"Dr. J?" Meg stiffened, anger creeping out from the cracks of her vulnerability. He had talked to her therapist? About her? Grip on her popcorn tightening, she turned to him. "Is that why you moved out and left all your stuff? Because *Dr. J* told you to?"

Austin stared at her, lips open and eyes wide in alarm. "No! Yes? Sort of?" he finished, tone coaxing. "We talked last week when she started you on that trial level of your new med."

Meg warmed, angry as she stood. She had entertained the thought that Austin had become a crutch as well. But now she wasn't sure if it had been her idea or her psychiatrist's. "You called Dr. J?" she accused hotly. "Austin, she's my therapist."

Her voice had gotten loud, and Austin pulled his gaze back from the quad, his worry that someone might overhear them obvious. "Well, who else would I talk to about you? You never tell me anything."

Kim Harrison

Flushed, Meg dropped back a step. Betrayal was hot in her. Austin and Dr. J both. "I can't believe you talked to my therapist," she accused. "Without me in the room. Behind my back."

"Meg…" Austin tried to pull her close, and she took another step away, furious. "It wasn't behind your back," he coaxed as he stood, his brow furrowed. "Come on, Meg. I would have told you sooner, but I didn't think it was that big of a deal. *She* called me. She wanted to know if I'd seen any of the side effects of that new drug she started you on, knowing how badly you wanted it and how easy it would be to fudge your answers. I asked how you were doing, and she said I was making it too easy for you."

"Easy?" Meg exclaimed, and Austin glanced at the trio of students crossing the park, his lips pressing into an angry line when they clearly heard her and began to laugh nervously. "You think this has been easy? My life is two steps to the right of hell, Austin. I have to fight every day to just manage what you take for granted. This isn't in my head!" she shouted, gesturing. "It's real. It's a struggle. You don't think I want to be able to drive to the mall without feeling as if I'm having a heart attack? Go out and catch a movie without freaking out? Have dinner without worrying that some nameless bad thing is going to happen? I'm glad you moved out. It saved me the effort of asking you to leave!"

Eyes narrowed, Austin took her elbow, his fingers curled and pinching. "Meg, I love you," he said tightly. "I only asked how you were doing."

"How I'm doing?" She tugged out of his grip. "Right now I'm mad as hell. If you wanted to know how I was doing, you should have asked me. Not made plans to move out because you thought it would be *good* for me." They had treated her like a child. A child!

"Okay, you're right." Austin's anger was easy to see, his jaw set tight. "I'm sorry."

But she couldn't tell if he meant it, or if he was only saying it to get her to shut up, and it only made her more angry.

"But Dr. J is right," he said, deciding it for her. "I'm a crutch."

"Yeah? Well maybe you should go, then," she snapped, arm wrapped around her middle.

"Maybe I will." He stared at her, an unfathomable thought making his shoulders stiff. "Enjoy your popcorn with your new friend," he finally said, and turning, he began to walk away, his limp painfully obvious. With a stiff motion, he threw his bag of popcorn in the trash in passing. Some of it spilled, and that scruffy dog came out of hiding and began to scarf it down, his tail tucked and his ears low.

"I will!" she shouted at his retreating back, but he never turned, never slowed. A surge of panic threatened, and Meg shoved it down, burying it in anger. He'd moved out because Dr. J told him it would force her to find a new level of confidence. Well, she was confident that she was pissed at both of them, and arm still around her middle, she sat at the fountain beside her purse. Head up, she glared at the trio of students going past, their steps fast and talking in nervous, hushed tones about their argument. It was all Meg could do to not tell them to mind their own business.

But slowly her anger eased, evolving into a relieved disappointment as the cool sound of the fountain reasserted itself. Scuffing her shoes, she looked at her phone for the time. Haley wasn't coming. Or maybe she had been and turned around and left after catching sight of all that drama.

"Did I just make a mistake?" she whispered, but damn it, Austin and Dr. Jillium should've included her in that conversation. She wasn't a child. She deserved the dignity of having had a voice in Austin temporarily moving out to encourage a new level of independence.

Besides, she mused as she miserably scuffed her shoes into the grit, maybe *she* would have rather moved out than Austin. She could have found her own place with lots of light and openness instead of being stuck in that brown hell they'd been living in for the past three years.

Again Meg looked at her phone. "She's not coming," she whispered. "I am such a fool."

Perfunctory **Af**fection

Standing, she miserably ate a piece of popcorn as she started down the sidewalk, back to her mac and cheese alone in front of the TV in her ugly brown apartment.

"Yoo hoo! Meg? Wait! Don't go. We're here!"

Meg spun, her popcorn spilling. It was Haley. A young man walked quickly beside her, the both of them little more than silhouettes in the darkness under the trees. *She didn't stand me up*, raced through Meg, then, *I hope they didn't see all that*. But it seemed as if they hadn't, and relief spilled through her, the last of her anger at Austin fading.

"I'm sorry we're late!" Haley called cheerfully, still at some distance away. "Rorry took forever to get himself in order." Her smile grew more distinct, her heels clicking on the pavers. "You know how men are," she added, softer as they closed the gap. "Always trying to impress someone or other."

Beaming, she held out a hand and took Meg's fingers in hers, pulling her into a quick hug. "You look nice," she said when she let go of Meg and hiked her large purse back up her shoulder. "Where are we going? I hope they kept our reservations."

"Thank you." Meg flushed, surprised at the hug. She had no clue where they were going to go, but she was glad she managed to have dressed herself appropriately. Haley had changed into a sweater and slacks as well, though hers was admittedly of a softer yarn than Meg's.

Kim Harrison

Nervous, Meg smiled at Rorry. He stood taller than Meg, and was dark where Haley was light. His black hair curled softly about his ears, and he was clean shaven. He wore a soft knit shirt and jeans with casual shoes. A smile played about his lips as he ran his gaze over Meg with an interest that was welcomingly casual, not carnal. He had Haley's angular chin, but his was stronger. If anything, they looked like siblings, not lovers, and Meg noticed they stood apart from each other a little.

"I'm so glad you waited," Haley gushed, taking Meg's hands again. "I realized half an hour ago that I didn't have your phone number. I am such a ditz. Aren't I, Rorry? He gave me bloody hell about it. We rushed over as fast as we could."

Rorry's smile became warmer, and Meg dropped her eyes. "A total ditz," he said, his voice low. "But it's part of your charm."

Haley beamed, standing between them as if eager to show Meg off. "Meg, this is Rorry. Rorry, Meg."

Meg extended her hand before Rorry could even try to give her a hug. "Meg Seton," she said, and Rorry took it, giving it a firm shake before letting go.

"And she *paints*," Haley said, as if proud of her.

Rorry winked at Meg, then cocked his head at Haley. "You told me that already."

"Yes, but she is really good," Haley said, as if that explained her enthusiasm. Then she hesitated. "Where's Austin?"

Meg's smile faded. "He had a family emergency," she lied. "He says he's sorry. Next time, maybe. Want some?" She held out the bag of popcorn, and Rorry eagerly helped himself.

"Oh." Haley's bright mood dimmed. "I hope everything is okay. Do you have to go? We're not keeping you, are we?"

"No, I'm good," Meg said with a forced cheerfulness, then just gave Rorry the bag to finish off. "He's got my number if there's a real problem, and I've got his." The last came out more grim than she wanted, but she couldn't believe that he'd gone behind her back. Moths had gathered about the fountain's lights, and as she watched, one got caught in the tiny spider's web, ripping it to shreds before falling into the water to drown, its wings too tangled to fly.

"Well, where will you take us?" Haley asked, and Meg jerked her attention from the doomed moth.

"Ah, I don't know," she admitted, and Rorry turned on a heel to look at the lights now flashing on the nearby building, the sound of the freshman mixer party becoming loud. "Austin and I usually spend Friday night doing something casual, like hot dogs and putt-putt golf." Meg flushed even as she said it. *Putt-putt golf? Did I really just suggest putt-putt golf?*

But Haley bobbed her head and looped her arm in Meg's. "The one just across the parking lot? I saw it this afternoon. I didn't know they had food. Let's do that."

Horrified, Meg was jerked into motion. "Oh, no." Meg scuffed her feet, trying to slow them down as Haley began to lead her across campus. "You wanted to go out to eat. All they have is hot dogs."

"It's Friday," Rorry protested as well, his attention on the unseen party. "It's a college town. There's got to be a club within walking distance. Or we could check out the mixer."

"With the freshmen?" Haley countered, looping her other arm in Rorry's so she was between them as she kept them moving forward. "I don't think so. Besides, golf is as good as anything else to get to know each other. Better, probably, since I don't have to watch you flirt with everything in a skirt and half of everything with a goatee."

Rorry flushed, and Haley confidently angled them toward the parking lot. "Besides, I'm not dressed for clubbing, and neither is Meg. I love a good hot dog."

"Haley…" Rorry persisted, neck craned to see the lights flashing on the building, and Haley turned to him, their pace never slowing.

"Yes, Rorry?" she said pointedly, and Rorry sighed.

"I love a good hot dog, too," he finally muttered, and Haley beamed, letting go of Meg just long enough to give him a loving pat on his chin.

"Lead on, Meg," she said cheerfully, the sound of the fountain going soft behind them. "I've got a mean bounce shot I want to show you."

Perfunctory
Af**fection**

"It's just past the parking lot," she said, relieved. This was as low-stress as it could get. That the "beautiful people" would want to do something she liked was more than gratifying, even if Rorry had suggested something more expensive and extroverted.

Happy, Meg smiled at the popcorn vendor as they passed him, surprised when he smiled back.

Six

"You go first on this one, Meg."

Meg's grip on the putter tightened. Her lips held a tiny smirk at Rorry's mild annoyance as she set her blue golf ball on the worn circle. The pleasant pattern of give-and-take that fifteen holes of putt-putt had created had left a surprising ease between her, Haley, and Rorry that made it seem as if they'd been friends for years.

Meg had won the last hole with a two-putt, which meant by Rorry's rules that she go first on the next. Behind her, Haley was adding up the scores, and Meg studied the classic windmill obstacle, the slowly moving fins blocking the direct line to the hole from time to time. This one had always given Austin trouble, but long practice gave Meg the advantage, and she tapped the ball while the fin was descending. By the time the ball got there, the way was again clear, and it rolled through unimpeded.

"Nice shot!" Haley said, looking sharp as she tucked the scorecard into her pocket.

Meg straightened from her putter's hunch, feeling good as she backed up to let Rorry take the tee. "Thanks."

Rorry's ball began to roll, and he impatiently set it back, gripping the putter awkwardly as he took his first swing. Meg winced, knowing before it moved that it was going to hit the next fin, and sure enough, it bounced back with a dull thud.

"Rorry, Meg just showed you how to time it," Haley admonished, and Meg tuned them out, looking over the brightly lit course as Haley began to give him pointers. They were in no hurry. The family ahead of them was taking forever at each hole, and besides, the point wasn't to get around the eighteen holes as fast as you could, but to enjoy the night.

And it was a beautiful evening. Meg sighed, content as she took in the elaborate putt-putt arena, busy despite the late hour with young families and couples testing the romantic waters. Spiderwebs glistened everywhere, attracted by the moths that beat their wings to tatters against the hot lights turning the course to noon. There was even a web in the fins of the windmill, and Meg wondered if the spider had spun it while it was moving or if it had been a surprise when the caretaker had turned it on this morning.

Perfunctory
Af**fection**

"Nasty things," Haley said, using the end of her putter to clear the web out before she sashayed back to the tee and set her ball. Rorry had finally made it through, taking three shots to do it. Haley, though, timed it exactly as Meg had. Her aim was better, though, and Meg caught her breath when Haley's red ball rolled, rolled, and finally dropped into the cup with a little thunk.

"Hole in one!" Meg shouted, and Haley grinned, returning Meg's high-five before sauntering around the windmill to supervise Rorry tapping his ball toward the hole—and missing.

"I'm no good at this game," he complained as Meg lined up her putt and sunk it.

"Austin and I come out here a lot," she admitted, her necklace swinging forward as she scooped her ball up and out.

The family was still lingering at the hole ahead of them, so Haley and Meg stepped to the side, watching Rorry smack his ball around, missing again and again.

"What is that? Six?" Haley said, then turned to Meg. "That is a beautiful necklace. Is that a real ruby?"

Startled, Meg picked it up, holding the pendant out to look at it on its silver chain. "Yes. Thanks. It's real. This one is an emerald," she said, pointing at the green gem set to look like a blob of paint on the tiny palette. "Diamond. Chocolate diamond. Sapphire. My mom gave it to me when I graduated art school."

Kim Harrison

"She must love you very much," Haley said, eyes solemn.

Meg let the necklace fall, resolving to clean it this weekend. She never took it off, and it looked tarnished under the hot lights. "She did," she said, feeling a faint heartache at the reminder of her mother's death. That was right about the time the anxiety started, stress that she was only now beginning to pull herself out of. "She passed a few years ago." It had been right before Austin moved in with her, trying to keep her grounded when her entire world fell apart.

"Got it!" Rorry called out. "That's seven for me."

"Nine," Haley countered as she wrote it down with that tiny pencil. "Seriously, it's just a game. Why are you lying about the score?"

"Why are you keeping one?" Rorry muttered as they moved to the next tee. "You should get a new necklace," he added, and Haley pulled up from having set her ball, giving him a smack with the back of her hand.

"It's from her mother," she admonished, and Rorry flushed.

"What..." he complained, gesturing at Meg. "It's full of bad memories. Look at her face."

"She's not getting rid of it," Haley intoned, giving him a dark look before settling herself before her ball. "I swear, Rorry, you are as sensitive as a slug. I think it's a beautiful expression, even if they are set in silver."

Embarrassed, Meg slipped the necklace behind her shirt, wondering what else the jewels would be set in. Gold? Her mother had been well off, but that would have moved it from extravagant to ridiculous. Meg never would wear it if it was gold, afraid of losing it.

The tap of Haley's shot was clear in the silence, and the ball sped cleanly around the banked curve and over the bridge, coming to rest two feet from the hole. Beside Meg, Rorry sighed. Meg was next, managing the bank and bridge, but her speed was too great and it bounced back almost into the tiny river.

"This might take a while," Haley said as Rorry hit his first shot badly, to make the ball bounce like a pinball before it stopped against the wall.

"That's okay. It's a nice night." Meg smiled up at the unseen stars. The moths were thick at the lights. She'd never seen so many. "Austin and I used to come out here almost every weekend."

"Used to?" Haley questioned as they waited. "Are you two having trouble?"

Alarm flickered through Meg, but it was based in embarrassment, not fear, and she shrugged. "I don't want to talk about it. I mean, I just met you. I'm not going to unload on our first date."

Smiling, Haley touched her arm in sympathy. Oblivious, Rorry swore as he finally made it over the bridge. "He'll come around," Haley said, shifting Meg's ball so Rorry's wouldn't hit it. "And if he doesn't, we'll find you a new boyfriend," she added as she rolled Meg's ball back.

"My shot?" Haley casually tapped hers in. "That's two for me. Meg, I think you're next."

"Hey! Don't think I didn't see you move Meg's ball," Rorry accused.

"Rorr, you are so far behind right now, you may as well be in Perfection," Haley said, unrepentant as she wrote down her score.

"That doesn't mean you can move her ball!" Rorry insisted. "Why keep track if you're going to cheat?"

"This coming from someone who keeps shaving strokes off his score?" she asked tartly. "And don't blame this on Meg. I'm making up for you double tapping your ball in on number three."

"I did no such thing," he protested, and smiling, Meg knocked her ball in, enjoying their banter.

It had become obvious that they weren't a couple. There was a loyal fondness, the feeling that they'd defend the other to the death, but the comfortable rivalry between them was too high to allow for romance. They teased each other more like siblings or long-time work associates.

"Two for me," Meg said softly, and Haley wrote it down.

"I could take the strokes from your worst hole and still beat you," Haley said calmly. "Actually, I will do just that if it will shut you up. Why don't you go first on the last one," Haley said, pointing to number eighteen.

Rorry lifted his chin, apparently satisfied. "I think I will. Thanks," he said, walking over to it in a huff. He set the ball on the tee, and it rolled off. Swearing, Rorry chased it down before it landed into the stream.

"You're not boyfriend, girlfriend, are you," Meg said when Haley dutifully changed her two to a twelve for her last hole, snorting at Rorry's ongoing frustration.

Haley looked up, her eyes wide in alarm. Behind her, Rorry's ball went up the hill and over the ravine, smoothly rolling to a halt inches from the cup.

"I'm sorry," Meg rushed, wondering if she had gone too far. "I mean, you just don't act like a couple."

"Ah, no. We aren't, actually." Haley winced. Behind her, Rorry was making an elaborate war dance around his almost-in ball. "We're just good friends. I would've told you, but two friends traveling around together sounds weird, so I tell everyone we're a couple. We never stay anywhere long enough for anyone to figure it out." Haley set her ball on the tee, brow still furrowed when she came back up. "You're not mad, are you?"

Meg shook her head, and Haley hit her ball, sending it easily over the ravine and down to roll within inches of Rorry's. "I'm not surprised you figured it out," Haley said as Meg took her place at the tee. "You're very perceptive."

Kim Harrison

"It's my artist's eye," Meg said. Breath held, she hunched over her ball and smoothly tapped it, sending it over the ravine to bounce around the confines of the green.

"My turn," Rorry said, rushing to sink his putt with a little tap. "Two for me!" he exclaimed, and both Meg and Haley cheered him.

But then he frowned, peering into the hole as he realized it was actually a tube that led back to the club house. His ball was gone, and, sighing dramatically, he stepped off the green, twirling his club like a saber.

"Sink this, and you'll win, Meg," Haley said as Meg lined up her shot. "Even if I hadn't taken ten strokes for Prince Loser over there. I want my dog with mustard and relish."

Smiling, Meg tapped her ball in. She looked up to see Rorry's reaction, but he was fencing with shadows. He was fun to be around, and if Austin was going to continue to act like a jerk, she might take the chance to get to know him better—seeing as Rorry and Haley weren't a couple.

Meg's ball went clunking and rolling back to the club house. Haley's was quick after hers, and Rorry came back, poking the butt of his club at Haley as she totaled their scores.

"Looks like you won, Meg," Rorry said without looking at the card.

Meg met his smile with her own, sorry to see the game over. "Then I'm buying. That's the rules. What do

you want on your dog, Rorry?" Meg looked at the food
cart parked forever in the parking lot. There were even a
few wooden tables under the bright lights, moths beating
around the lamps.

"Ketchup," he said, handing his club over when Meg
gestured for it. "And a lemonade."

"Haley?" Meg prompted, taking her club as well to
return to the club house. "What do you want to drink?"

"I'll just have some of his," she said, beaming as she
handed Meg the score card. "Don't forget to get your free
game for the hole in one."

"You got it. Meet you at the table."

The world seemed to be spinning right for once, and
Meg felt good as she took the clubs back to the little hut. She
tucked the score card in her purse instead of turning it in for
a free game, not wanting to ever forget the few hours spent
in the warm night under electric lights. Mood bright, she
went to get their food.

It was only when she was standing in line that she realized she hadn't had one twinge of anxiety all night, and a
curious sense of peace seeped up through her soul, reminding her what it felt like to be normal. The only difference
was Dr. Jillium's meds, and hope that this might last settled
deeper into the bedrock of her soul.

She knew her happiness was still there on her face as she
turned to see Haley and Rorry waiting for her at the table,

needing to reassure herself that they were still there. Haley was carefully wiping the table free of spider webs and dust, Rorry cheerfully getting in the way. Maybe next time she could try to go clubbing. She wouldn't have to dance, just sit at the table and watch.

"Ma'am?" the vendor asked, bringing her attention back.

Meg smiled as she recognized the overweight and cheerful man wiping his hands off on his apron. He was as much a fixture as the fiberglass bear and kiddy slide. "Three dogs, two with mustard and relish, one with ketchup," she said, adding, "And a large lemonade and peppermint milkshake." The milkshake was tradition, and her mood tarnished at the thought of Austin. He loved peppermint, and sharing the large milkshake was the highlight of their evenings.

Clearly pleased with himself, the man set a tall, frosty paper cup on the counter. "I've already got your shake ready. I saw you on the last hole and figured you'd want one."

Meg's smile widened. *He remembered me?* "Thank you," she said as she took it, grabbing two extra red spoons in case Haley or Rorry wanted any. "Mmmm, perfect," she said as she tried a bite. "As usual."

Grinning, the man bobbed his head. "Give me a sec for the dogs."

He dropped back into his cart, and Meg turned to look out over the parking lot to the dark night beyond as she scooped out a spoonful of cold peppermint. The vendor guy was being really nice to her. The woman in the club house had talked to her differently as well. It had to be Rorry and Haley. Haley was so bright and outgoing, filling a room and making everyone with her seem better than they were. As the peppermint milkshake settled cold into Meg, she wondered for the first time if maybe Austin not being here was a good thing.

With an almost desperate gratitude, Meg watched Haley dramatically wave away the moths, but Meg's smile faded as her focus shifted to follow a furtive movement at the shadows. It was that scruffy dog, and her back stiffened as he trotted to that homeless man and begged for something from a paper bag.

Lips parting, Meg took a breath to call out, hesitating at the last moment. Haley might think she was a nutcase.

But still, the idea that Christopher might be following her trickled down Meg's spine, triggering a flash of anxiety. "Not this time," she whispered as she hurriedly popped one of her new pills, chasing it down with a spoon of milkshake.

Pulse fast, she stared at him from across the parking lot as he searched the trash barrels for cans, willing him to go away. She wasn't going to ruin the chance of a friendship by being afraid of a homeless man, even if he was wanted by the FBI. *Maybe I should call Daniel*, she thought. But if

Daniel showed up, she'd have to explain to Haley why he was here.

The beep of the register shocked through her, and Meg spun, eyes wide. Their food was ready, and she dug her card out from her purse. "Thanks," she said when she noticed the man had put everything in a paper tray for her, smiling as he pushed it across the counter. Her breath came easier when she turned back to the parking lot and both the dog and man were gone.

Maybe he was just looking for cans, she thought as she made her way to the table, pausing to grab napkins and straws.

Rorry was sitting with his back to her, his dejection clear as he probably moped about losing. "It's not too late to hit the dance club," he said, and Meg's smile faded, the harsh paper rough on her fingertips as she pulled a napkin from the dispenser. "Come on, Haley, this is lame."

"Excuse me?" Haley said caustically, and Meg jerked to a stop, feeling as if she'd been hit in the gut. But then Haley added, "Meg is *my* friend, not yours, you selfish twat. I'm having a great time. Not everyone wants to watch boobs and asses bounce up and down in time with the music."

"Awww, come on, Haley," Rorry coaxed. "That's not what I meant." He touched her arm, and Haley looked up, her gaze jerking over Rorry's shoulder to Meg. "I want to be here. Really."

"Meg!" Haley exclaimed brightly, and Rorry turned, not a shadow of his disappointment on him. "Wow, that was fast."

Meg came forward and silently slid the tray onto the table between them. Haley had stood up for her, but she didn't like the idea that Rorry had only been tolerating the evening. That she'd read him wrong bothered her. "Yeah, they're pretty quick around here," she said as she sat down, a new distance between them.

"They look great." Rorry took his ketchup-smothered dog in hand and quickly lost himself in it. "Thanks, Meg," he managed around his full mouth, then grunted in appreciation as the bug-zapper popped. "Dude, that had to have been a June bug."

Haley was a little more delicate, taking her hot dog and sliding from Rorry to sit right across from Meg. "I am *so* glad I ran into you this morning," she said, eyes closing in appreciation as she took a bite of her hot dog. "I wouldn't know where to get bodacious dogs, or a good game of putt-putt if I hadn't."

"I'm glad you're having fun," Meg said, but it was hesitant, a new uncertainty coloring her thoughts.

"I had a great time." Stifling a yawn, she arched her eyebrows and drew her hot dog close when Rorry asked if she was going to finish it. "It's getting late for me, though. I'm usually in bed by eleven."

"Me too," Meg said, though she seldom called it a day before one in the morning. The thought that Haley was trying to slip away so she and Rorry could go dancing took a stronger grip. That two such beautiful people actually *liked* spending Friday night playing putt-putt was unrealistic. They were both too perfect.

"I've had a lot of fun," Rorry said, and Meg winced, hearing the beginnings of a graceful get-away. "We'll have to do it again. Maybe not on a Friday, though," he said, then jumped when Haley nudged him under the table.

"Hey, if you're not doing anything tomorrow, I could use some help finding an apartment." Haley dabbed a stray bit of mustard off her lips. "I usually take a month to look around and find the best spot, but anyone who knows where the best hot dogs are probably knows where I could find a place with lots of sun." Haley's gaze jerked to Rorry when he cheered a big moth hitting the bug zapper. "Two bedrooms, on campus if possible," she added dryly.

Meg nodded, a whisper of relief easing her mood. Haley, at least, had enjoyed herself. Otherwise she'd never ask for her help. "Sure. I don't have anything planned." Tomorrow was Saturday, and all Meg had on her list was to call Austin and apologize for blowing up at him. Yes, he had talked to Dr. Jillium about her behind her back and moved out without telling her the truth about why, but he'd only been concerned about her.

"Great!" Haley waved a moth away, her annoyance at it obvious. "Is seven too early?"

For a Saturday, it was, but Meg nodded as she finished her hot dog. If they were getting together early, then Haley and Rorry were not going to spend the rest of the night clubbing, and the feeling of belonging began to grow again. *Grow up, Meg. No one is lying to escape your presence.* "Seven is fine."

Haley beamed. "Super. You are the best, Meg. I'll never be able to pay you back."

"It's not a big deal." Meg sipped her milkshake, easy now that it had melted somewhat. Again her thoughts turned to Austin as the minty frost slipped into her. Maybe Dr. Jillium was right. He was a crutch, and she wasn't going to sit here drinking a milkshake that had always been more his thing than hers. "Either of you want the rest of my milkshake?" she asked as she set it down and pushed it away.

"I do." Rorry enthusiastically reached for it, his straw squeaking as he pulled it from the lemonade and dropped it into the shake.

"Garbage gut," Haley said as she wadded up her paper wrappings.

Thin eyebrows waggling at her, Rorry took a long pull at the straw. Gagging, he shoved the cup away, turning to hack and cough.

"Ice cream headache?" Meg asked, but he'd hardly gotten any into him, and Haley bent close, a hand on his back.

"Rorry? Rorry!" Haley demanded, and Rorry looked up, grasping for his napkin to wipe his mouth out.

"Peppermint," he managed, face red and eyes tearing. "Who puts peppermint in ice cream?"

Haley's eyes widened. A look of horror came over her as she stared at the almost empty cup. With an eerie quickness, she rose, and, using two hands, carried the cup to the trash and threw it away.

Shocked, Meg sat and blinked until it dawned on her. "Oh, crap. You're allergic to peppermint? I'm so sorry," she gushed. "I should have asked, but I've never heard of anyone being allergic to peppermint. Are you okay? Should I call 911?"

"No!" Haley rushed, then softer, "No, he'll be fine. He just doesn't like it is all."

Rorry gave Haley an ugly look as he slammed what was left of their shared lemonade, making faces as he swished it around before spitting it out onto the grass.

"Are you sure?" Meg asked. Great. *I make a new friend, then poison him.*

"He's fine. He's being a drama dude." Still standing beside him, Haley gave Rorry an annoyed smack on his shoulder. "Suck it up, big man!"

"I did," Rorry warbled. "And look at me."

"Serves you right for not asking what's in it." Haley's hand slid from Rorry. "You're not going to die." Turning, she

Perfunctory Affection

laughed at Meg's crestfallen face. "Seriously, he's okay. Soon as Mr. Snowflake is done, we'll walk you home."

"I'll be fine," Meg said, not wanting to make anything worse. Honestly, Rorry looked as if he'd swallowed pureed brussel sprouts. "It's just across campus."

But Haley shook her head, her focus on the dark beyond the electric lights. There'd been no new people starting a round of putt-putt, and it was emptying out fast. "No," she said as her gaze came back. "I saw a vagrant wandering around earlier, and I'll sleep better knowing you got home okay. Besides, I need to know where you live if I'm going to pick you up tomorrow to go apartment hunting," she said brightly. "We can have breakfast first, my treat."

Still wiping his mouth out, Rorry added, "She won't take no for an answer. Trust me on this. Just say yes."

"Then I'll say yes," Meg said as she stood to take her and Rorry's trash to the can, but the memory of Haley's horrified expression when she threw away the shake hung with her, making her feel as if she'd done something drastically, almost irredeemably wrong.

Seven

A thin, unexpected slice of light made it into the kitchen at six thirty in the morning. Meg felt like a starving child hidden under a banquet table as she sat in it, still not fully awake but functioning as she waited for the coffee to kick in—black, no sugar, no milk. The mug was warm in her hand, the nutty scent of it doing as much to wake her up as the shocking bitter taste of it slipping down.

Smiling at the simple pleasure, she looked out the tiny window over the sink that opened onto the brick wall of the adjoining apartment building. It felt empty and quiet at this hour, the street deserted and the apartment seeming to belong to someone else. She was merely taking up space, like one of Austin's SF figurines or his gaming console.

Mood souring, Meg ran her thumb over the jewels set in her necklace, thinking they felt like braille dots as she remembered Rorry's comments about it making her sad and Haley's staunch, oddly possessive remarks that Meg was *not* going to get rid of it.

Grimacing, Meg dropped her necklace. She still felt embarrassed for having nearly poisoned him. Haley had been positively repulsed as she'd thrown it away. Maybe they didn't have peppermint in Perfection. She'd have to ask Haley while they apartment-searched.

A tiny trill of excitement traced through Meg as she reached for her phone and the list of furnished apartments she'd made up last night after Rorry and Haley had walked her home. They were all on campus so they wouldn't have to get a car unless they wanted to. Most were in good locations and away from the worst of the university's frat and sorority houses, though Rorry would have probably preferred being right in the thick of them. Haley could pick out her favorite three or four right from Meg's phone over breakfast, and they could be done by noon.

"As long as I don't forget to take it," she whispered to herself as she dropped her phone into her purse waiting for her on the kitchen table. It slid out of sight under her still-empty diary, and Meg ignored the guilt. She hadn't had time to write in it last night, busy with making Haley's list.

Rising, Meg took her empty mug to the sink and rinsed it out. Her shoulders slumped as she dried her hands on a towel, wincing at the brown sameness of it. Austin's things looked even more ugly now that he wasn't around to use them. That Haley might want to come in when she came over to pick Meg up filled her with a near terror. Somehow she'd managed to convince Haley that she was friend-worthy even with a night of putt-putt, but that would change if the classy woman ever saw the inside of her apartment.

"Something has to change," Meg said, her voice loud as she hung the towel up, despairing at the faded dullness of it. The dishcloths on Austin's space-remake show had always been pristine-white sackcloth, sporting whimsical designs that showed the homeowner's playful side. All she had were frayed tan that Austin had gotten cheap somewhere before they'd met. *Why haven't I changed them? It's been three years.*

Lips pressed, she vowed not to call him today. It wasn't any of his business where she was or who she was with. Agitated, she spun the pinky ring he'd given her. Maybe after a little silence on her end, he might appreciate her more.

Chin high, Meg pulled the brown towel from the rack and, with a firm conviction, threw it away. Pulse fast, she tugged her purse closer, digging through it until she found the bottle of pills Dr. Jillium had given her. Shaking them all into her hand, she counted them, funneling all but one clattering back into the bottle before capping it. She'd thought she had more than that. There was hardly enough to get her through the weekend.

Kim Harrison

Filling her coffee mug with tap water, she took her pill. Head down, she stood in the slice of moving sun as she waited for it to take effect. That Dr. Jillium had talked to Austin behind her back grated on her, but she didn't want to lose access to her meds. It wasn't as if she could just change psychiatrists and get a new prescription.

Brow furrowed, she found her phone. She could leave a message with Dr. Jillium about how she was doing with her homework and that she might need to come in Monday for a new batch of pills. *Six forty-five*, she noticed as she scrolled through the short list of contacts and hit call.

It rang once, and Meg took a breath, exhaling when Dr. Jillium answered, not the expected voice mail.

"Meg. Is everything okay? Where are you?"

Surprised, Meg exhaled. "Ah, I'm great. I was expecting your answering machine is all. I'm sorry to be bothering you this early on a Saturday."

"I was up," Dr. Jillium said. "Is everything okay?"

"Yes." Wondering at the woman's worried tone, Meg inched deeper into the vanishing sun. "I just wanted to let you know that last night was the best night I've had in three years."

"Oh, Meg, I'm so happy for you," Dr. Jillium said, her relief obvious. "You talked things over with Austin, then?"

She hesitated, her anger seeping back into her. "Not exactly. I took a woman I met on campus out to play putt-putt." *My God, it sounds so lame when I say it like that,* Meg thought, putting a hand to her forehead.

"That's even better," Dr. Jillium said as if Meg had done some great thing. "I'm looking forward to hearing about it when you come in."

The brush-off in her voice was clear, and Meg panicked. "Can we move my appointment to Monday?" she asked, trying to keep the urgency from her voice. "I'm going to be out of pills by Friday."

"Oh." There was a slight hesitation. "You're taking four a day, then?"

Arm wrapped around her middle, Meg pressed back against the wall and into the shadows. "You said I could. They're working. I'm not seeing any of the side effects. Everything tastes the same. I fell asleep fast and didn't wake up even once. No rashes."

"No, it's okay," Dr. Jillium said, and Meg tried to ease the breath from her so the woman couldn't hear. "If nothing changes over the weekend, I can certainly give you a new bottle Monday."

"Thanks, Dr. J." Meg slumped against the wall, eyes closing. She didn't want to go back to the way things were. "This is amazing stuff."

"Just so you know that it's you making amazing strides," Dr. Jillium said. "It's not a magic pill. Tell me about your new friend."

Meg's lips twitched in annoyance at the sudden, clinical tone. The woman was fishing to make sure Meg wasn't lying about her progress to get more meds. "She's a guest teacher. I'm helping her find a new apartment today."

"Is Austin driving you?" she asked, and Meg's anger flashed to a slow burn.

"No." Meg opened the drawer beside the sink, staring at the clean brown dishtowels waiting to be used. "She wants to be on campus, so we're walking, I assume. She doesn't have a car either." Eyes narrowed, Meg threw every last brown dishtowel in it away. "I'm kind of mad at Austin right now. Did you really ask him about how I was handling the Fitrecepon and that he should move out because he was a crutch?" Her pulse raced at the hint of anger she let color her voice—just a hint.

"Meg," Dr. Jillium coaxed. "I didn't tell him to move out. You know I can't do that."

Meg frowned, sure she had couched it so it would seem like it was his idea. "No, you were right," Meg interrupted breezily. "He is a crutch. But I would've liked to have been in on that conversation instead of having things decided for me as if I was a child."

"I'm sorry this happened," Dr. Jillium said, and Meg hated her cool, calm voice, always in control, always judging her. "Fitrecepon is highly experimental. That you continue to metabolize it well is important. We've had issues in the past, and your health is my main concern."

Perfunctory
Af**fection**

Meg was silent, the phone feeling hot in her hand.

"Meg," Dr. Jillium coaxed. "I'm embarrassed to be having this conversation over the phone. Please believe me when I say that there won't be any more conversations with Austin without you there."

"I don't think that will be an issue anymore, anyway," Meg said tightly. Leaning against the kitchen sink, she took a long, slow breath and stared out at the brick wall. "I love him, and he loves me, but you're right that I've been using him to avoid moving forward. I can't keep doing this."

"Possibly," Dr. Jillium said, and Meg frowned, never having allowed herself to do it when actually in her psychiatrist's office. "Meg, don't do anything out of hand. Fitrecepon impacts your brain in subtle, deep-set ways that are not always easily apparent."

"Fitrecepon is not responsible for Austin talking about me behind my back," Meg said boldly. "Him making decisions for me that we should be making together."

"True, but it might be a part of why you're so angry with him," Dr. Jillium said. "You're doing wonderful on it, and after such a long time of being down on yourself, even a little confidence can make you feel unstoppable. Fitrecepon isn't a maintenance drug. It's to jump start positive patterns that will allow you to permanently alter your behavior. I don't want you to make any changes that you're going to look back on and regret."

Meg tried to slow her emotions, well versed in what medication could do, both good and bad. "I hear what you are saying," she said, but her eyes were on the pills in her purse. She couldn't imagine not taking them. Not yet.

"I want you to come in on Monday, okay?" Dr. Jillium said, and even though that was why Meg had called her, an uneasy feeling took root. "I'll have a new prescription for you, and we can devote the entire hour to you and Austin. He cares very much about you."

Meg grimaced, willing to bet that her new prescription wouldn't be as potent. "I know. I love him, too," she said softly. "I'll try to get him to come in." But she already knew that Austin wouldn't step foot inside Dr. Jillium's office. She'd tried before. For someone who was enthusiastic about her going to therapy, he was adamant that he didn't need any.

"Certainly."

Meg's gaze flicked to the shifty-eyed cat clock over the archway to the living room. Haley would be here any moment. Just the idea of having her knock on the door and ask to come in made Meg's stomach knot. "Thanks, Dr. J," she said, trying to end the conversation without looking like she was. "I'll see you Monday."

"Have a great weekend." Dr. Jillium seemed to be in no hurry, and Meg leaned over the sink to try to get a glimpse of the sidewalk. "Keep up the good work with your diary, and call me immediately if anything changes."

Perfunctory
Af**fection**

"I will." The beep of the phone disconnect was a relief, and Meg leaned farther over the sink. But the sidewalk was empty, and she rocked back to her heels. Again her eyes went to the empty diary, and she vowed that as soon as she and Haley were done this afternoon that she'd write down when she'd taken the Fitrecepon. The first one was at class, one at the fountain, one at the putt-putt, one this morning....

The sun was gone from the kitchen. Purse in hand, Meg went to sit by the living room window where she'd be able to see Haley coming long before she got to the door. She'd go out to meet her on the sidewalk and circumvent a tour of her drab apartment entirely.

But she stopped, frozen before the window when she saw Christopher at the row of mailboxes.

Meg's breath caught. Her pulse hammered, and she didn't move, knowing if she did, that he'd see her past the long brown curtains. *Daniel Hun*, she thought, never taking her eyes off the man at the mailboxes as she fumbled to find his card in her purse. Then she hesitated. Haley was coming. She couldn't ask her to hang around so she could tell a man from the government that she'd seen the guy he was looking for. Haley would think she was a loser.

Christopher looked up. Meg's eyes widened, her grip tightening on the card. *He sees me*, she thought in near panic, but then he turned, wedged something into her mailbox, and walked away.

Meg inched to the window, breathing easier when she saw him halfway down the street, yelling at a car that nearly hit his dog. Her eyes flicked to the mailboxes. Curiosity burning, she found her mailbox key.

The sun on the raised walkway was almost a shock, and holding her keys like a claw, she made her way to the mailboxes, wondering how it could be so bright outside, and so dull in her apartment. A quick look up and down the street assured her Haley wasn't here yet and Christopher was gone. Key rasping, she opened the mailbox to find a torn square of newspaper.

Puzzled, she flipped it over to see it was a coupon for an Asian eatery. "What the hell?" she whispered, studying it as she locked her box back up and turned to go back inside. A coupon?

"Can you see them yet?" a raspy voice asked, and Meg jerked to a halt, terror slicing cleanly through her.

He was standing there, between her and the stairs, that yappy dog in his arms and a wild look in his eyes. His hair was matted, and he looked as if he hadn't shaved in a week.

"What do you want?" she asked, dropping back a self-preserving step. "I saw you last night at the putt-putt course. Are you following me?"

Christopher took a step forward, and she gasped, retreating to the sidewalk. His clothes were filthy, and there were no socks between his feet and dirty sneakers. A white, institutional-looking tee was tucked into his baggy, long pants, and it and the red plaid shirt he wore over it looked splattered with something that might have once been red. *Blood?* she wondered, becoming more frightened. She could smell him from where she stood, sort of a swampy, burned-leaves smell that caught at the back of her throat.

"Have they asked you to go with them?" he asked, eyes hidden behind dark sunglasses as he struggled to keep the dog in his arms. "It's not too late. Not for you."

"Get away. Go on!" she demanded loudly, scared to death as she gestured wildly, as if he was a squirrel or cat, but it was early, and no one was walking their dog or taking a run to hear. The street was deserted.

Christopher put up a hand as if trying to reassure her, and she scrambled back almost to the pavement. He'd escaped from a hospital. Who knew what he would do? Frantically looking up and down the street, she kept retreating, hoping he'd follow enough that she could get around him and back in her apartment.

"You're a patient of Dr. Jillium," he said, struggling with his wiggling dog, and she stopped stone cold in the shade of the old oaks. "Throw them out before it's too late. Can you see them yet? Can you!"

The last was a pained shout, and she shook her head to humor him. "Leave me alone," she whispered. "Stop following me."

"I'm trying to help you," he said, but she didn't move when he came forward another step. "I'm Christopher. Or at least I used to be until I was in one of Dr. Jillium's trials. I know she's giving you Fitrecepon. Can you see them yet? It might not be too late."

"See what?" she asked. Two more feet, and she could get around him, and she fidgeted, her heart hammering hard enough to burst.

"Not what. Who!" he shouted, gesturing in frustration. "Them!"

My God, he has totally lost it, she thought, eyes widening. Breath held, she rushed to get past him, panic making her heedless. "Let go!" she shrilled when he caught her arm. "I'll call the hospital!" she shouted as she shoved him, and he pinwheeled back, grabbing her arm to keep from falling. "Let go. Let go!" she exclaimed, fighting for her balance.

The dog was on the ground, barking wildly as she hit his arm holding her. But he wouldn't let go, and she took a breath to scream. Someone would come. They weren't all hung over.

"Daniel? You talked to Daniel?" the man rasped. Eyes wild, he let go. Meg lurched back, heart pounding. "Oh, God. You can see them. Don't call him," he begged, cowering as he backed away, his little dog getting tangled in his feet. "He's not from the government. He works for Dr. Jillium. He wants to take me back to Perfection. I can't go back there. I'm not crazy. Stop taking the pills. Throw them out. Meg, it's not real. None of it is real."

He knows my name, she thought, chilled hearing it coming from someone she didn't know. "Stay away from me," she whispered, scared but not as much as he was, his eyes wide and his expression drawn.

"Throw them out," he said, falling to a knee to try to catch his dog. "They're flesh dealers. They want you because you have something they can't do. Do you sing? Tell stories? Are you good with games?"

He'd finally gotten his dog, and he stood, clutching it so hard it squirmed to escape. They had switched places, Christopher cowering almost in the street, her standing more confidently on the sidewalk to her apartment. Confused, she hesitated, her panic sliding from fight-or-flight to a more enduring fear of being in a danger she couldn't yet see. Head high, she refused to let it take a grip on her, but the familiar anxiety settled in as if it belonged, and maybe it did. Maybe this fear was all she was.

"No," she said, but then went cold when she recalled how Haley had liked her painting. She'd seemed almost proud of it when she'd shown Rorry.

"They tricked me," he said, voice low and raspy as he crept closer. "They lied. I thought it was heaven, but it was hell. I escaped, but it will be harder now. You have to throw them away. Now!"

"Leave me alone!" she insisted, inching back to the stairs. That Haley liked her work didn't mean anything. Half the art faculty had commented on it. This guy was nuts, and if she listened to him, he would make her nuts, too.

Wiggling dog gripped tight, Christopher looked furtively up and down the street. "They make you feel as if you're one of them. That you can be perfect, but it's a lie. You can never live up to their expectations. You'll never be more than a clever pet." He staggered, the dog slipping from him as he stared down the street with an open-mouthed fear. "Oh, God. It's her."

Shocked, Meg followed his gaze, seeing nothing. She jerked at the scuff of his shoes, but it was only Christopher running away. She watched his awkward gait, the dog silent at his heels as they slipped between the parked cars and were gone.

"Crazy ass," she whispered, heart still pounding. She looked at her apartment window as she thought of Daniel's card in her purse. The fruit loop was AWOL from a mental hospital. He knew Dr. Jillium, or at least her name. Worried, she decided she'd ask Dr. Jillium on Monday. Daniel had said he was unstable, and Dr. Jillium had warned her there were more severe side effects other than itchy skin and things not tasting right. The woman had been almost paranoid about making sure Meg wasn't showing any signs of a bad reaction. *Paranoia and*

Perfunctory Affection

hallucinations? Meg wondered, arms around her middle as she started back inside.

"Yoo hoo! Meg!" a lightly feminine voice called distantly. "Isn't it a beautiful morning?"

Meg spun, her planned morning rushing back. It was Haley, still a block away, looking like a cover model for a woman's magazine in white capris, red top, and a white, wide-brimmed hat in her hand. Sandals scuffing noisily, she walked down the sidewalk with a casual grace, her blond hair catching the light that peeped through the thick oaks.

Meg looked down at her own jeans and light weight black sweater. *At least I don't look like a tree-hugging art teacher,* she thought disparagingly. "Hang on. I'll be right back. Let me get my purse. I've got a list of apartments all ready to check out," she called. She'd change, but then Haley would want to come inside.

"Meg, you're just the best!"

Waving Haley to stay where she was, she took one last look at the street before dashing upstairs and into her apartment. Her pulse was fast, not because Haley might have seen that ugly confrontation if she'd been two minutes sooner, but that she desperately didn't want Haley to follow her in. Nothing was going to ruin today. Not a protective boyfriend, not a worrywart psychiatrist, and not some guy who was wacked out on way too many meds.

Eight

"It was so nice of you to make a list of furnished apartments for Rorry and me," Haley said, her voice bright as her low-heeled sandals clicked smartly on the sidewalk. "I would have just gone on some lame website and ended up with a drab hole in the wall under a family with four kids and a dog."

"I don't mind. It was fun." Haley's steps were exactly in time with Meg's softer scuffing, and it made Meg feel special.

"I can't tell you how much I appreciate you doing this with me," Haley continued, her words so fast it seemed unlikely that she even heard Meg. "Rorry says thank you, too. I mean, a single woman, going to look at apartments in a new town? He is such a worrier. He'd come himself, but he's out doing errands."

Meg watched Haley's perfect, red-painted toenails, moving with a hypnotic rhythm. She'd never had her toenails painted except once for a wedding. "It's not a problem," Meg tried to wedge in, but Haley hardly slowed to take a breath.

"Rorry couldn't stop talking about last night. I know he complains a lot when he's not the center of attention, but he really did have fun. He's always so serious. It did him good to do something that had no meaning but for spending time with people you like."

Serious? Meg thought, then looked up, surprised to find Haley squinting to make her look vulnerable. "I like spending time with both of you, too," Meg said, and Haley's smile widened.

"I can't tell you how glad I am that you stopped to help me yesterday," Haley said, then abruptly stopped. "Here we are! I've got a reservation."

Meg's attention rose, her smile fading as a sick feeling rose up from her gut. "S-Swanks?" she stammered, embarrassed. It was the nicest restaurant on campus, the place where you went with your family when you got your doctorate or were entertaining the president of the United States, maybe. Meg couldn't go in there. Not in blue jeans and no makeup. Haley might be dressed for it, but she wasn't. "Uh, I didn't know they served breakfast," she said, sneakers solidly planted on the sidewalk as Haley practically floated to the door.

"They do if you're staying here." Stunning in her crisp outfit, Haley waited, her hand on the door.

Perfunctory **Af**fection

Meg's eyes traveled up the four-story edifice to linger on the foreign flags. They were staying at the University Rail? *Of course they are. Probably the top floor.* "I can't go in there," Meg said, fingers playing with her necklace nervously.

Lips pressing impatiently, Haley's touch on the door fell. "I told you, they serve breakfast if you have a room."

Haley began to push the door open, and Meg took a step forward, not wanting to be left behind even as her palms began to sweat and her head to hurt with the beginnings of a migraine. "Haley, I'm sorry, but I'm not dressed for it. I thought we were just going to meet for coffee before going apartment hunting."

Haley jerked back from the open door. The scent of fabulous coffee and the sound of a live harp drifted out before it slipped shut behind her. A slight frown marred her perfection as she stood on the stoop and looked Meg up and down as if only now really seeing her. "I wanted to thank you for your help today," she said as if that was all that mattered. "Coffee isn't going to do it."

Meg took an imploring step closer, feeling as if everything was about to crash down to a jumbled rubble of "should've, could've." But she could *not* go in there, and her heart beat faster as panic began to pool in her. "I'm not… dressed right," she said, gesturing at herself as something very close to shame rose. She was a hick, a backwoods, one-room school teacher compared to Haley's cosmopolitan polish and tastes. "There's a coffee shop just a block down," she said, warming. "They won't be busy on a Saturday until noon, and they have great apple turnovers."

"Apple turnovers?" Haley echoed, and a new embarrassment filled Meg. She and Austin had shared one every Saturday morning, but under Haley's scrutiny, the quaint tradition seemed vapid.

Meg clenched her purse, suddenly more scared of losing Haley's friendship than the ugly looks she might get inside. "Or we can eat here," she said, voice breathy and panic swallowing her.

"No," Haley said, and Meg's eyes shot to hers, looking for, but not seeing, disappointment. "The coffeehouse is fine, but I'm going to get you into Swanks before the weekend is out, Meg. Even if I have to take you shopping to do it."

Shoulders easing, Meg breathed a sigh of relief as Haley joined her on the sidewalk. Swanks was a nice idea, but one that wouldn't happen. Haley was silent as they continued down the sidewalk, and guilt slowly pushed out Meg's relief.

"I'm sorry," Meg said, imagining she saw a hint of annoyance in Haley's sudden, bright smile.

"No, I should have told you my plans," Haley said, but her pace wasn't as brisk, and it made Meg feel even worse.

Meg lurched to get the door for Haley when they got to the coffeehouse, and Haley went in before her, the woman's expression empty as she scanned the nearly empty tables and tall ceilings that had always made Meg feel comfortable. "This is nice," Haley said, staring at the barista who was ignoring them as she played something on her phone. "There's a table there in the sun. Why don't you claim it?" she added, but it was more of a demand than a request. "I'll get the coffee. What do you want to eat?"

"I'm fine," Meg said, though the thought of one of those apple turnovers made her stomach pinch. "Haley, I don't mind getting my own coffee."

"You won't let me do anything for you, will you," Haley protested. "You treated us to putt-putt last night. The least I can do is get you breakfast. You sure you don't want something?" She leaned to look into the cold shelves. "Ugh. Apple turnovers. I can't stand apples. All mushy paste. Wait, they've got lemon tarts," she added, her mood brightening. "You want one? That's what I'm going to have."

Meg looked into the case. The apple turnovers looked luscious with gooey frosting dripping down and a light, flakey crust that Austin would have tried to snitch from her. There was no way she was going to have one now. Shoulders slumping, she eyed the dull yellow tart. "Why don't you grab that table by the window? I don't mind getting breakfast if you want to get lunch," she said, and Haley's bright expression faded. "I just want coffee," she explained. She couldn't eat her usual apple turnover in front of Haley. Coffee would do.

Beaming, Haley gave Meg's arm a squeeze. "Deal. Can you get me one of those double caramel frappés? And maybe a lemon tart?"

Meg nodded, her attention flicking to the man making a beeline to the counter to slip in ahead of them. "Sounds good." Meg gave him a disparaging look. "Go sit down. We don't both have to stand in line, and that way, doofus there won't take the table we want."

Haley snorted her agreement, the delicate sound making Meg smile even more. "Good idea, and thanks," she said, giving Meg's arm a touch before sauntering to the table in the sun and grabbing a few napkins along the way.

An odd feeling of disconnection was beginning to take hold as Meg settled in behind the man now ordering a labor-intensive ice-and-fruit drink. The hum of her phone drew her attention, and she fumbled for it, shoulders rising when she saw it was Austin, texting her to find out where she was.

OUT WITH HALEY, she texted back, still mad at him.

She jumped when her phone rang in her hand, her grip tightening as she stared in annoyance at his name glowing on the screen and remembered when she couldn't wait for him to call. Now, she wasn't sure if she even wanted to talk to him—not when she was still trying to decide if she wanted to break up with him. She did, but Dr. Jillium might be right that it was the meds making her hasty.

Perfunctory **Af fection**

I am going to make myself crazy. Meg took a slow breath, finger hesitating over the accept button. He had stuck with her through the worst of her panic attacks. She knew it hadn't been easy. Austin had come into her life when everything was at its worst, reminding her that things would get better and that someday she might be entirely free of it. Not to mention very few people would be willing to watch her cart around her emotional baggage until she found the ability to leave it by the side of the road.

"What can I get you?" the woman behind the counter asked, and Meg let the call go to voicemail.

"Two double caramel frappés and two lemon tarts, please," she said, suddenly needing to share something with Haley more than the pleasure of eating what she really liked. Her palms were sweating as the woman punched it all in, and Meg finished up with the card reader while she got the pastries.

Haley was at the table when she turned, the classy woman wiping the crumbs to the floor with a napkin and evaluating the results with a careful scrutiny. A shaker of cinnamon was sitting on the table as if it was a centerpiece, clearly taken from the nearby coffee bar. Fidgeting, Meg played with her necklace as she waited, jamming her phone to the bottom of her purse so she wouldn't hear if Austin called again.

"Here you go," the barista said, and Meg jumped, dropping her necklace as two large coffees and a bag with the tarts were slid across the counter to her.

Kim Harrison

"Hey, can I have a second fork?" Meg asked, and the woman jerked to a halt in her rush to help the next person. Eyes rolling, she added another plastic fork, and Meg took it all.

Turning, she exhaled as she found Haley settled in the sun, looking like a modern-day goddess with her head down over her phone. She'd half expected the woman to be gone. "Coffee and tarts," Meg said as she approached, and Haley, quickly hid her phone in her purse sitting on the chair beside her.

"Oooh, you got a caramel frappé too? You're going to love it with the tart," Haley predicted, but Meg just sighed as she sat down and looked into her coffee. It was a pale tan, full of milk and probably too much sugar. "It's even better with cinnamon," Haley added as she shook some from the shaker. "Rorry loves his with cinnamon," she said as she shook even more into Meg's cup.

Meg dutifully took a sip, stifling a shudder at the thick, almost syrupy texture. It could hardly be called coffee. "Mmmm, great," she lied, and Haley carefully tore the bag to make it into a plate of sorts.

"Isn't it to *die* for? It pairs up excellently with the tarts." Haley's gaze was on a woman across the street, walking her dog. "I love my dessert coffees." Eyes bright, Haley delicately chose a tart, her nail polish gleaming as she angled it to take a tiny bite, completely ignoring the plastic fork. "Mmmm, this is good. I hope I didn't get you up too early."

"No, it's fine." Shunning a fork as well, Meg mimicked Haley and picked up her tart, warming at the black paint in her cuticles, and that her nails were too short to ever be considered pretty. As expected, the tart was a sugar bomb, and Meg's chewing slowed as she wondered if it was going to curdle the milk in her coffee and give her a stomachache. Maybe that's what the cinnamon was for. But Haley had been so nice that not eating it wasn't an option. Trying to get rid of it, Meg took a huge bite. She washed it down with a gulp of coffee, shuddering at the sickening sweetness.

"I had no idea that the sun made it into my apartment this time of year," Meg said, and Haley's attention came back from the street.

"Oh, I did get you up too soon," she gushed, hand reaching to touch Meg's atop the table. "I'm sorry. God, I'm so selfish. You've been so nice to me. You have no idea how hard it is to be moving all the time. You have to be so bright and perfect to make friends, and you've been so wonderful. I feel as if I can relax around you and just be myself."

Her perfect, perfect self, Meg thought, taking another bite of the tart. If she worked at it, she might get it all down in four gulps. "No, I should be the one thanking you. I'd have nothing to do today if you hadn't asked me to help you find a place." Nothing but sit around in that brown apartment, that is. She could paint for only so long. Eventually she had to come up for air to eat and sleep—and the world would be there, waiting for her.

Haley eyed Meg over the rim of her coffee. "Is Austin still being a dick and not apologizing for whatever he did?"

Meg blinked in surprise, then smiled, but it faded fast. "It's not him. It's me," she said, but this time, it was true, and she pushed the tart crumbs together into a little hill, avoiding the last piece. "I might be outgrowing him. I don't know. He moved out a few days ago," she admitted. "And my apartment is empty of him and full of him all at the same time. I can't tell if I miss him, or if I just don't want to be alone. It doesn't help that that vagrant you saw last night was stuffing coupons in my mailbox this morning."

Haley set her coffee down, her brow furrowed in concern. "Are you serious? Right outside your apartment? Goodness. Maybe he's a fired postal worker that went postal."

Meg laughed. She didn't really want to talk about it, and that she'd opened up even this much left her uneasy. But everyone had trouble with their boyfriend now and again. That it was because he talked to her psychiatrist behind her back didn't need to enter the conversation. Haley was so together, she didn't even *need* a boyfriend. She wasn't afraid of anything.

Frowning, Meg shoved the thought away. "I've got three good options and four maybes lined up this morning depending on how close you want to be to the center of campus," she said, head down as she dug in her purse for her phone. "I emailed them all last night, so they know we're coming over sometime today to take a look. The sooner the better because two furnished rooms go fast. I'm surprised there's even any out there."

Pretty and lucky both, Meg thought as she scrolled through her phone and brought the apartment app alive. A map of campus decorated with little blue flags popped up, and smiling, she turned it so Haley could see.

Haley brushed her fingers off and reached for the phone. An oddly vulnerable look made her perennial smile seem forced. "Meg, Rorry is going to be gone for a few days starting tonight. If we find a place today, why don't you stay over? Help me move in, maybe?" she asked.

Meg froze, a thrill of belonging racing through her.

"Just until he gets back," Haley rushed, clearly mistaking Meg's deer-in-the-headlights stare. "It more fun shopping with someone else. I've done it alone so often, it's almost a chore. Please say you'll come with me?"

"Um, I don't want to impose," Meg started, remembering the awful feeling of being out of her league as she stood on the sidewalk at Swanks.

"Impose? I'm asking you!" Her smile warm and real again, Haley gave Meg's hand a squeeze. "And as I said, Rorry will be gone tonight. We could take a few days. Do a girl's weekend shopping. I've seen furnished apartments before, and furnished doesn't mean finished." Haley let go of Meg's hand, her eyes rolling. "I could use some help picking out everything to make it look homey and nice. And to tell you the truth, it would make me feel better with someone else there the first couple of nights. I'm not superstitious, but I don't like to be alone. And with that vagrant wandering around playing postman, you shouldn't be either," she finished, eyebrows bunched to make her look serious and pretty both.

"You want me to help you pick out your furnishings?" Excitement sifted through Meg, then dread. What if Haley didn't like what she suggested?

"Pillows, rugs, plants. There's no way to go wrong with any of it." Haley blotted up the last of her crumbs from the napkin and ate them off her finger. "Oh, tell me you will," she added, plaintively. "It will burn Austin's britches when he finds out that you don't need him as much as he thinks. Can you imagine his face if he stops over and finds you gone? All weekend?"

Meg began to smile. Burn his britches? It would at that. Dr. Jillium would be pleased that she was doing something out of her comfort zone. And frankly, she needed to get out of that apartment. Meg couldn't make up her mind while she was surrounded by him, even when he was gone.

Perfunctory **Af**fection

"It sounds like fun," she said, and Haley almost jumped up and down in her chair. "If we can find a place today, I don't see why not."

"This is going to be wonderful!" Haley gushed, then drank the last of her coffee down in one go. "What's the first place on the list?" she said, startling Meg when she shifted to sit beside her so she could see her phone better. "We can get you some new shoes while we're out. Something to wear into Swanks. My treat. I won't take no for an answer. I owe you dinner, now, not just breakfast."

Meg felt light, her stomach knotting from the sour tart fading into nothing as Haley pressed close to see, the woman completely oblivious to how special she was making Meg feel. "I thought we could start with the one on Liberty," Meg said, the sweet coffee tasting better every time she sipped it. "There won't be any morning sun, but lots in the afternoon."

Nine

I f there was one word to describe Haley other than perfect,
it would be focused. The heels of the confident woman's
sandals clicked smartly as she came out of the front bedroom, her boundless energy beginning to make Meg feel
tired. "The bathroom needs some updating, but it's clean,"
Haley said, her expression intent as she probably compared it to the last three apartments. "Hardwoods and tile
throughout. Very workable. Just needs a few rugs to brighten
the place up." She hesitated under the dated chrome light
hanging over the Formica table, frowning as she brushed a
cobweb away. "And maybe an exterminator."

"The spiders are bad this year," Meg agreed.

Haley's grimace deepened. "I'll take your word on that."

Tired, and hungry, Meg sat on the arm of the heavy
leather chair set before a conspicuous empty spot.
Furnished apparently didn't include a TV. If it had been

Meg's decision, she would've taken the first place they'd looked at, rating it enormously better than the dim dungeon she lived in now, but Haley was picky, and it was likely they'd be spending all afternoon looking at the last three on the outskirts of campus.

"Still, there's enough room in that back bedroom that Rorry could set his desk up right in there." Haley turned to the wide sliding glass doors that led out to a narrow, paint-chipped balcony. "I wouldn't have to look at his clutter over dinner. That would be a nice change."

With a decisive motion, Haley turned on a heel, hands on her hips as she studied the faded furniture in the living room. "Cover that ghastly couch with a nice print, add a few pillows to dress it up... My desk would fit in that corner. I wouldn't have to worry about the sun wreaking havoc with my screen way over there. But I imagine that if I painted, I'd want to be right at the windows. Look at that sun coming in!"

Meg nodded, already having rated the sun as an A plus, plus. It was a spectacular place to paint, out of the way and in the sun, a bright corner to spread out in with lots of light. "It's better than my artificial light," she said, hoping Haley didn't hear the envy in her voice.

"Maybe the other bedroom is bigger." Haley strode across the living room and vanished into the second bedroom. "Hey!" her voice floated back. "This one has a door right to the balcony!"

Perfunctory **Af**fection

Meg exhaled long and slow, her lethargy taking a stronger grip. Her feet were in the sun, and she looked over the light-strewn apartment feeling relaxed and sleepy. It was all she could do to not settle deep into the leather chair in the sun and take a nap. Haley was running her ragged. The remaining apartments were on the outskirts of campus, and Meg wasn't looking forward to either the long walks or the bus rides to get there.

If it was Meg, she would take this one. The apartment had an open concept living space and a balcony large enough to grill on. The kitchen overlooked the living room and then the quad beyond. Being the fourth floor up and the top level, there'd be little noise from neighbors. There was no elevator, which was probably why it was still available.

That, and maybe the spiders, Meg thought, watching one making a web on the outside of the large sliding glass door where the evening light would bring in the moths. "I could live here," she whispered, liking the open brightness, high up and away from everything dark and ugly.

"What's that?" Haley said, a tiny pink tape measure in her hand as she came out of the second bedroom.

"It's a nice apartment." Meg forced herself awake as Haley stood before the window walls and took in the view.

"You can see everything from up here," Haley said. "Do you think there's enough room out there for a grill? It's been ages since Rorry and I have had a place where we could cook outside."

Meg rose and went to stand shoulder to shoulder with Haley. The wide balcony would be a fantastic place to paint even with the traffic noise. So much sun. "I would think so," she said. "If you put it in the corner, there's even enough room for a small bistro table and chairs."

Why hadn't she and Austin found a place like this instead of that dark brown hole good only to hide from the world in? But maybe that's what she had wanted three years ago.

"Can you see me out here after class, relaxing with a glass of wine?" Haley said wistfully. "Able to watch everything and not have to be right down in the thick of it?"

They sighed at the exact same moment, and laughing, they both turned away. "And how about that kitchen?" Haley wandered into it, opening cupboards and drawers. "It's the perfect size, don't you think? I'd only need to get a few bright hand towels, maybe a set of colorful canisters for decoration." Her eyebrows rose. "Or a chicken!" she said excitedly. "Wouldn't that be whimsical? We could decorate the entire kitchen with chickens. Bring the barnyard theme right out into the living room with rustic furniture and chicken wire."

Country? Meg thought, surprised.

"Not the couch, of course, but end tables, country throw rugs. Keep the picture frames old barn wood. Maybe a barn-wood coffee table. Chic. Very rustic chic."

Perfunctory **Af**fection

Ah, Meg thought, realigning her thinking. *Shabby chic.* It wasn't country at all.

"Rorry could have this thing," Haley finished, giving the metal and glass table a sidelong tap with her foot.

"That would look nice," Meg said, envious as she saw it with her mind's eye. Why couldn't she could live here in the sun?

"Do you like it?" Haley said, almost bursting, and Meg nodded. "Me too." Exhaling happily, Haley came out of the kitchen, her eyes traveling over the room's lines. "I don't need to see those last three. I want this one," she said, and Meg's shoulders slumped in relief. "I'm going to take it. Right now. Before anyone else does. Rorry will love that back bedroom, and I like the sun."

"That's great," Meg said. "I'm so glad you found something you like," she added, feeling the unusual exercise to her bones. But now there was shopping. Surely Haley would want to take a break first, maybe get some lunch.

"I'll be right back." Haley gestured for her to stay. "I'm going to nail this shut. Where did the manager say he was?"

"A1?" Meg sat on the arm of the chair again, glad the apartment hunt was over but not looking forward to an afternoon of shopping right on its heels. All those people. She hadn't been to the mall on a Saturday in years. What if she had a panic attack while they were trying to get a pretzel or something?

"A1," Haley echoed, her expression showing her delight. "Hang tight. I want to get some drape measurements before we head for the mall."

Focus distant, Meg spun her pinky ring as she wondered how she was going to handle the next few hours. Then she started, surprised when Haley gave her an expansive, quick hug, smiling as she dropped back to run her gaze over the apartment again. "Thank you, Meg. I *never* would have found so nice a place if not for you. We're going to have to go out to celebrate at Swanks tonight. I'm getting you a new dress to thank you, so no excuses!"

"Swanks?" Meg echoed, a new feeling of panic welling up. It was too much. She had to take a break.

But Haley was already at the door, key in hand as she went into the hall. "This is going so well. I'll be right back!" she called. And then she was gone.

Hands shaking, Meg dug into her bag to find her phone and check the time. Guilt flickered as she brushed past her empty diary, then relief when she found her phone and realized it had been four hours.

"I can do this," she whispered as she found her pill vial and almost fled into the kitchen for a glass of tap water. Hands shaking, she filled a dusty glass and popped a pill. If Haley could find an apartment in the morning, furnish it in the afternoon, and then go out to eat at night, then she could too.

Perfunctory Af**fection**

Setting the glass in the sink, Meg wiped her chin. Her hands were no longer trembling, and she exhaled in relief. The view was nice even from the kitchen, and thinking that it would take Haley some time to sign the rental agreement, she went back to the living room and collapsed into the cushy leather chair—now that it was Haley's.

"This is harder than it should be," she whispered, but she could do it if Haley was beside her. She made Meg feel stronger, able to handle anything, and Meg began to smile. Dr. Jillium would crap her pants if she walked in on Monday and told her she'd gone to the mall on a *Saturday*.

Leaning forward, Meg watched a couple throwing coins into the fountain. If Haley could find her a pair of shoes and a dress for tonight, and if they sat in a corner where Meg could look at the wall with her back to the people, she might be okay at Swanks.

But then Meg's smile faded as she recognized Austin's distinctive walk, stomping his way across the quad.

What is he doing out here? she thought as she stood and went to the window, and in a flash of anger, she put a hand on the door, contemplating going out and yelling at him from the balcony. He was going to ruin everything if he came up here and Haley saw them argue.

Lips pressed, she rummaged in her purse to find her phone. He'd left three messages, but none of them explained why he was following her. Suddenly she felt cornered, her anger swinging back to panic when he angled toward the building. He *was* looking for her. She'd told him she was going apartment hunting with Haley, and there were only so many available.

My God, has he checked them all? she thought, then grimaced. No, not all. Just the ones on campus.

"Haley," she whispered, purse in hand as she looked at the door to the hall. He would meet Haley if she hid up here and did nothing. The last thing she wanted was to have a boyfriend meltdown in front of Haley. The fear of losing Haley was strong, and, purse in hand, Meg hustled out of the room, breath held all the way down the four flights of stairs.

The tiny lobby was empty of Haley or Austin both, and relieved, she pushed out through the double glass doors and onto the sidewalk. The bright light after the dark stairway was blinding, and she squinted, her back stiffening when she saw Austin on the other side of the street, waiting to cross. He paused when he caught sight of her, then jogged across, his partially fisted hand held to warn the oncoming traffic that he wasn't going to stop.

Angry or not, Meg stiffened when a car whizzed narrowly behind him, not even slowing. "Are you following me?" she shouted before he was halfway across, and his attention jerked from the offending car to her.

"You didn't answer my texts," he shot back, his worried look marred by annoyance.

Perfunctory Affection

Arms over her middle, Meg stood before the door of the apartment house as if she was guarding something precious inside, and maybe she was. Haley was everything she wanted to be, and she wasn't going to let Austin ruin it. "I was busy," she said, and Austin halted before her, that irate expression on his still-stubbled face.

"Out with Haley. Right," he said, then scrubbed a hand over his face, all but one of his fingers curled under to hide their thinness caused by disuse. His anger had vanished to leave only a faint worry. "Meg, I looked her up last night. There isn't anyone named Haley in the university directory."

"There wouldn't be because she's a guest lecturer and she's new," Meg said defensively. "It took them six weeks to put my name in. Have you been checking the rental listings looking for me? That's called stalking, Austin. What do you want?" Her palms were sweaty, not so much for standing on the sidewalk and yelling at him as much as her worry that Haley would come out and find them there.

But Austin was in no hurry to leave, his weight on one foot as he scowled up at her, seeming like an entirely different person as he reacted badly to her new independence. "Maybe if you would read one of my texts, you'd know I was trying to see if you were free for lunch." A thin smile turned him back into the man she usually saw. "I couldn't stand the thought of you sitting in that dark apartment all day. I thought we could go play putt-putt. Maybe have a milkshake."

Suddenly their traditional night out seemed tame and vapid. "I already made plans with Haley. Sorry," she said stiffly. She'd die if Haley caught her drinking another peppermint milkshake, and she wasn't going to tell him they were going to the mall lest he follow them there.

Austin's weight shifted to his other foot. "Bring her along. I'd like to meet her."

You had your chance yesterday, and you blew it, she thought, very sure she didn't want them to meet. He'd ruin it, say something wrong and Haley would realize what a dweeb she really was and be gone. "We're going out for lunch. Maybe some other time. Let me know if you want anything from the apartment, okay?"

Meg warmed at her harsh brush-off, but she was still angry with him, and the sooner he left, the sooner she would breathe easier. Clearly feeling it, Austin rocked back, his hands moving as if he didn't know what to do with them. "Meg, I know I made a mistake, and I'm trying to apologize," he said as he reached out for her.

Meg pulled back, knowing if he touched her, her anger would vanish, and she liked feeling this empowered. "No," she said shortly. "You're stalking me. Go away."

"How is this stalking?" Austin's brow furrowed again. "How can I be stalking you? We share an apartment."

"No, we *shared* an apartment," she said. "You moved out."

"Temporarily, sure, but not out of your life." Austin hesitated, as he searched for the right words. "That's why I left all my stuff. Why do you think I'm standing here? It was supposed to help you," he said, frustrated.

"You know what would help me?" Meg's chin lifted. "You turning around and walking away for a few days. Give me a chance to make up my mind, because if you keep pushing, my answer right now isn't going to be one you like."

"Make up your mind? About what?" he asked, and then he paled, understanding that she was considering breaking up with him for good. Standing before her in his jeans and casual tee, Austin seemed to deflate. "Meg, I'm sorry. I'm only trying to help, but something is wrong. I… I think your new meds are too strong."

A spike of fear pulled through her, and then she shoved it away. "You said you wouldn't talk to Dr. Jillium behind my back again," she accused, and Austin held out a hand in placation.

"I haven't!" he protested. "But you're not yourself, Meg. Look at you. Out all morning. I called at six thirty, and you were already gone."

Meg relaxed at his plaintive tone, her hand behind her back fiddling with her ring. "I had an early coffee date. And my meds are fine. They're working just fine," she said again to convince him. "If nothing was different, then there'd be a problem."

"Yes, but you're too different," he said, voice softer as he moved closer. "Can you take a step back, slow down a little? I'm not telling you to stop, just ease up for a day or two. If it's real, it will still be there when you stop."

Stop? Was he crazy? She backed up, startled when her shoulder hit the door to the apartment building. "My God, Austin. I'm glad this happened. I think you liked having a broken doll to play with," she said bitterly.

"That's not fair." Austin's expression became hurt. "I want you to be better, but it's too much, too fast. You're seeing new people, doing new things that normally you wouldn't even think to try. I'm happy for you, but when change happens this fast, it's not growth, it's…a side effect. You aren't you anymore. You've changed."

Meg's focus shifted, a quick motion drawing her attention over Austin's shoulder. It was that damn dog of Christopher's, and her brow furrowed. He was a mess, hallucinating his fears into existence and unable to function outside of a hospital. But that was before they'd known the early symptoms of a bad reaction. Dr. Jillium was being careful. It wouldn't happen to her. "I thought changing myself was the entire point," she said, attention coming back to him when the dog ran off after a squirrel.

"Change, yes, but this?" He gestured to her, and Meg looked down at herself, seeing nothing she didn't like. "It's too much."

"Good, because who I was before sucked." Meg stiffened as she heard Haley calling her name clear through the heavy glass doors. Suddenly flustered, Meg felt for the handle. "I have to go," she said, fumbling to back up and not let him follow her. "Stop stalking me, or I'm calling campus police."

"Meg, wait!" Austin exclaimed. "Can I call you later? Where are you going this afternoon?"

She edged in around the glass door, holding it shut against him. "No, and it's none of your business." Breath fast, she pushed it closed, praying he didn't follow her as she ran back up the stairs, knees weak.

She and Haley were going to go shopping at the mall. It would be busy, but she could handle it if Haley were beside her to distract the attention away from Meg. They were going to turn Haley's new place into something bright and beautiful, a place with no clutter and nothing that reminded her of who she'd once been. Something perfect.

Ten

Meg held her breath as the stylist sprayed a light mist to "tame the flyaways." She watched through squinted eyes as the woman artfully finger-curled a few strays, her expressive face smiling at the result. It smelled light and clean when Meg took a cautious breath, nothing like her mother's hairspray, and her shoulders relaxed. At her feet, the woman giving her a light pedicure was just finishing up, rolling Meg's pant legs back down and giving her knee a little pat. Her toes were now a soft mauve to make her feet look as if they belonged to someone else.

"All done," the woman said as she stood from her rolling stool and pushed her cart away. "Don't move for at least ten minutes."

Pleasantly tired after an afternoon of shopping, Meg sighed. "No problem."

"Well?" The stylist handed Meg a mirror and slowly spun her so she could see the back of her head. "What do you think? It's a lot lighter with the layering. I think it suits you."

Meg angled the mirror, not recognizing the back of her head. Her curls had been tamed into smooth, glistening waves, and she shook her head to make them sway. "I love it," she said as she brushed a lock hanging before her eyes. It was softer than she expected, making her feel pretty.

"It's a versatile cut." The stylist turned Meg back around and took the mirror. "I promise it will look good with a wash-and-wear, too. Spend a little attention, and you get fabulous!"

"It is amazing," Meg said, truly stunned at what the woman had managed. "Thank you so much." Eyes fixed on herself, she shook her head again to feel the waves cool against her neck.

"It was my pleasure." With a flourish, the stylist took off the drape.

Meg smiled in delight as the basic-black drape was whisked away and the true impact of the last hour in a chair were revealed. Her black hair was a dark accent against the colorful new V-neck top that she and Haley had found before hitting the home furnishing stores. The soft fabric was cut tight to show off her small chest and narrow waist, and it went well with the black capris, new as well. Seeing it all together with her updated hairstyle, she dreaded the thought of putting her sneakers back on. Not when she looked this good. Haley had found everything on the just-in rack, convincing the woman to let her wear them out for their afternoon of shopping entertainment.

"Sit tight," the stylist said as she gave Meg's shoulder a light touch. "Your toes aren't dry yet. I'll see if Emily is available to do your nails. You want the same color, yes?"

"Yes please." Meg glanced at the nearby rolling rack. The array of bright reds, purples, and even golds were daunting.

"How's your coffee?" the woman said as she put her curling iron away. "Need a refill?"

"No, I'm good." Meg took her paper cup of tan coffee from the nearby counter and raised it in salute. She took a sip as the stylist click-clacked away. It was sweet. Haley had made it for her, and she was beginning to get used to the sugar overload.

"That neutral is a good color on you," Haley said from her perch on the nearby, vacant stylist's chair, her head down over her phone. "You were right not to go with the red. It would have drawn too much away from your dark presence. But that shouldn't surprise me." Her head came up, smiling. "You have a great eye for color. Must be an artist thing."

A wave of belonging went through Meg, almost painful from its long absence. Grateful, she set her coffee down as Haley texted someone, her own bright red, newly polished nails flashing. "I really appreciate this," Meg said, wiggling her toes at Haley. "But if I get my nails done too, they're just going to get ruined on Monday at class."

"Then they will look fabulous tonight." Closing her phone down, Haley smiled brightly and recrossed her knees. She was sitting sideways to look like a fashion model, and again Meg wondered why the woman was spending the day with her. "Let me do this for you, Meg," Haley said as if reading her mind. "It's the only way I know how to say thank you. And my God, you look great. I knew there was a real beauty under the artist. There always is." Getting up, Haley came to stand behind her, leaning so that both their heads were together as they looked at their reflections. "Wow. We look great," Haley said, and Meg felt herself warm.

"I can never repay you," she said, flustered.

Haley drew back, eyes still on Meg's curls as she smiled. "For what? No, this is my treat. I want to, and it's my pleasure. Besides, we're going to look fabulous when we walk into Swanks tonight. Reservation for two, all set."

Haley patted her back pocket where her phone lay, but Meg's flutter of anxiety quickly evolved into anticipation. They *would* look fabulous. She could hardly wait to put on that skimpy, gold-silk dress that she'd bought between the tin mixing bowls and chicken potholders. It was so light, it was like wearing nothing.

"You are *not* going to put those sneakers on over your new toes," Haley said, abruptly swooping down to pick them up where they sat beside the pedicure cart. "You can wear your sandals out." Holding the sneakers with two fingers as if they were dead rats, Haley took them to the register where their things lay piled and began searching.

Meg smiled and looked away, wondering how Haley was going to find her new sandals among everything else. Pleasantly exhausted, she was content to sit and be pampered, knowing she would fall asleep fast tonight with nothing to keep her awake.

She and Haley had hit all her favorite stores, the ones she never got into but knew their entire stock from the catalogs that failed to brighten up her dull apartment. Between Meg's knowledge of what they had and Haley's willingness to spend money, they'd outfitted the small apartment in an afternoon. Haley was a power shopper, and what sat beside the door was perhaps only a third of what they had bought. The rest was scheduled to be delivered on Monday.

Her new dress hanging behind the counter in a protective bag had been last-minute. Haley had practically dragged her into the high-end clothier, soundly beating the saleslady in a snob-down before pushing Meg into a dressing room and throwing three yellow and gold evening dresses in to her. Meg appreciated having been spared the torture of trying to find something suitable. All of them had fit perfectly, thanks to Haley's expert eye, accenting her narrow

Kim Harrison

hips and modest bust to make her sleek and slim. Confident. Feminine in a way that said power. Meg had only needed to pick her favorite. It was far away and distant from her usual earth tones, making her feel like someone else as she had stared at herself in the changing mirror.

And I'm going to wear it tonight at Swanks, she thought, touching her soft waves again.

"Good Lordy," a masculine voice said from the store's waiting area. "Is that Meg?"

Meg flushed at Rorry's voice. Full of a pleased anticipation, she spun her chair to see him in the threshold of the spa as if reluctant to enter without an invitation. "I thought you were gone for the weekend," Meg said, and Rorry came in, giving the receptionist a slight nod. A faint thread of dismay pulled through her, even as she was glad to see him. She wasn't going to spend the night with Haley if Rorry was there, and even as she thought it, her dismay shifted to worry. That loon, Christopher, knew where she lived, and Meg's eyes dropped to her purse next to the stylist's counter. She could call Daniel, but it had been twelve hours, and he probably wouldn't come out.

"I am," Rorry said as Haley joined him and gave him a quick peck on the cheek and a bland side hug. "But the commute home is unpredictable and tends to break down. I'm aiming for tonight, but I was *not* about to get involved in Haley's decorating. Not after last time." His attention slid

146

to the pile of bags, and he actually shuddered. "But it seems that I'll be her pack animal despite my plotting."

Haley beamed, giving him another squeeze before sliding away. "We could use your help. Thanks for coming to get the stuff," she said, and Meg silently nodded, now knowing who Haley was texting earlier. "Can you imagine us trying to lug all that home on the bus?"

"Yes." Rorry sourly looked at the pile again. "I can. But I came anyway because I wanted to see Meg. Wow." Smiling in appreciation, he looked her up and down. "You look amazing. Love your toes."

"Thanks." Still flushed, Meg took her sandals as Haley extended them. "It's Haley's fault."

Rorry grinned. "It usually is."

Haley gave his shoulder a backwards smack with a good-natured sourness. Chuckling, Meg dared to put her sandals on over her still tacky toes, marveling at how pretty they were.

"Hey, this means we've got an apartment," Rorry said. "I can't wait to get out of that hotel room. Key?" he asked, hand outstretched, and Haley reached for her purse.

"I need this back after you're done lugging everything over there," she said as she handed him the thick key still holding a paper apartment number tag. "*Before* you leave, Rorry. I don't want to get stuck trying to explain things to the manager again."

"I'll stop and get a new one cut," Rorry promised as he pocketed it. "Maybe two," he said, grinning at Meg.

Meg's head snapped up as Haley's eye twitched.

"Stop it," Haley said, sounding annoyed. "Meg and I are just having a girls' weekend while you're gone. Meg has her own life." Her brow furrowed, Haley sat on the adjacent stylist's chair again, knees crossed. "Though I'll admit I'm glad she's going to be with me tonight. That horrid man we saw at the putt-putt is lurking about. Did you know someone from the government is looking for him?"

"Daniel?" Meg blurted in surprise. She'd been so careful not to mention him around Haley.

But Haley's shoulders slumped in relief, and she reached across the space and touched Meg's hand as if needing the support. "He talked to you too?" she said, eyes pinched. "Clearly the deranged man has a type. It's probably a good idea we're both staying somewhere he doesn't know about. With some luck, he's already back in custody, but until I know for sure, I'd sleep better if someone else was in the apartment."

She thinks we're a type? Meg thought, her concern for Christopher vanishing in a swirl of belonging.

"So, Meg." Rorry leaned against the stylist's counter. "How did you ever get her to settle on one place so fast? It usually takes forever."

"It was the light," Meg said immediately, and Haley nodded her agreement. "The living room has sun from noon on.

You're going to love it. I'm surprised you didn't want to go apartment hunting and have a say."

Arms going over his chest, Rorry looked at Haley. "She never listens to what I want," he said softly. "Sun in the living room, huh?"

Haley chuckled and took a sip of her own coffee, her gaze on the nail stylist still finishing up with her client. "There's sun in your room. I'm not looking at your desk over dinner anymore."

"See what I mean?" Rorry's lips twitched, and then Meg watched him pack his annoyance away. "I can't wait to see it," he said, his attention going to the pile of bags beside the door. "Really," he finished with a half sigh. Then he brightened. "Haley, I want to give it to her now. Before I leave."

"Rorry!" Haley exclaimed, looking not afraid exactly, but maybe affronted?

"Why not?" Rorry coaxed. "It will go with her new dress better than that old chain of silver she has on."

"Give me what?" Meg asked, then turned to Haley. "When did you tell him I got a new dress? When?" But the real question might be *why* did she tell him she got a new dress.

"When you were trying them on." Haley looked a tad uncomfortable. "I called him to come and get the new stuff for the apartment. If he doesn't want to go shopping, fine, but I'm not going to lug it all home by myself. That you were trying on dresses came up in conversation." Brow furrowed, she turned to Rorry. "Rorr, it's too soon. She's going to think we're crazy."

Rorry pushed himself away from the stylist's counter. "No she isn't," he said, but a hint of dismay colored his usual upbeat mien. "It's just a necklace."

Meg felt a stirring of worry as Rorry reached into a front pocket and drew out a length of delicate gold chain, a heavy, fractured stone pendant weighing down its center. "Oh, it's beautiful," Meg said in awe as she took it, unable to help herself. The bright lights in the salon lit the stone as if from within, the smooth finish of the teardrop shape a startling contrast to the broken look of it as cracks radiated out from the center. "I've never seen anything like it. What kind of a stone is it?" she asked, knowing that she could never accept it.

Rorry pressed close, clearly pleased. "Do you like it? It will go better with a gold dress than your silver necklace."

He had crouched to put his face beside hers to look at it, and regret that she was going to give it back was heavy in her. "Rorry, I can't accept this," she said, wincing when his expression fell. Behind her, she heard Haley mutter "I told you."

"It must have cost a fortune," Meg said, trying to put it into Rorry's hands, but he had backed up, his worry obvious. "I've never seen anything like it, but I can't accept it."

"I told you it was too soon," Haley grumbled.

Rorry took it—only to undo the clasp and put it around her neck. Her curls were a soft tickling whisper, and she froze, the sensation going all the way to her toes.

"It didn't cost a fortune," Rorry said. "I want you to have it. It's as unique as you are, and it belongs around your neck."

Meg stared at herself in the mirror, her hand going up to touch the stone still warm from Rorry's pocket. It fell just below her mother's necklace, the smooth, fractured stone at the nadir point. "It's beautiful," she said, loving the way it looked, even if her neck was cluttered with both of them there. "But really, I can't accept it. I just met you two."

"You ruin everything," Haley said, her frustration looking old on her. "You know that, Rorry?"

Rorry's smile faded. "I'm... It's just a necklace," he protested, his crestfallen expression making him look as if he'd done something wrong.

Guilt seeped into Meg, and she began to fidget. "Rorry, it's okay," she finally said, thinking Rorry's embarrassment was worse than her guilt at the clearly expensive present. "Thank you. I love it."

Relief filled Rorry as Meg put a hand possessively over the stone and she effectively accepted it. "You do? You'll keep it? I'm so glad," he gushed, and Haley arched her eyebrows, still disapproving of Rorry's innocence. "I wish I could be there tonight to see it on you. Haley, take a picture tonight, promise?"

"Okay." Haley said. "Are you sure you don't want to come to dinner with us?" she asked, but her tone said for him to back off.

Meg's fingers fell from her new necklace. She would've liked to have him see her all dressed up.

Everything clearly right with the world again, Rorry looked out into the busy mall. "No. I'm going to wait for my commute. If I don't make it tonight, I'll have to wait until morning."

"That's too bad," Haley said, but Meg could tell she would be glad to be rid of him for a while.

"So, where are you going?" Meg asked. "Home?" Her mother's necklace looked dull and faded beside Rorry's gold dewdrop, and she frowned at it.

"Yep." Distracted, Rorry fiddled with the cart of nail polish. "Perfection. I can't wait. It's been almost a year." Eyes alight, he looked at Meg. "The air is so clear, you almost drink it, pooling in your lungs like light itself. And at night, the sky turns pink and gold and purple when the sunset reflects off the mountains. Never the same colors twice. In the winter, there are more reds, and in the summer, golds, but always purples."

"It sounds beautiful," Meg said. *They live near the mountain?* she mused, having no idea where. Their faint accent was totally unfamiliar.

Haley cleared her throat, and Rorry quit touching the nail polish to lean back against the stylist's counter and look tall and sleek, his gaze oddly distant. "When the conditions are right, the ocean reflects it all, and it's like you're living in heaven," he said with a sigh.

"Wow. Oceans and mountain both?" she said thinking it sounded European. "Lucky you."

"I bet you could paint it," Rorry said, and Meg's smile went faint. Her new style didn't lend itself to colors and shapes that the eye wasn't already expecting, but she might be able to do something banal with her old techniques.

"Maybe someday," she hedged, and Rorry beamed.

"Rorry…" Haley warned.

"Sorry." Rorry pushed himself up. The light in his eyes was utterly gone.

"It's not the kind of place you can get to with a passport," Haley said as she came forward to put a hand on his shoulder. "Rorry, can I talk to you for a moment?"

Irritation crossed Rorry, then vanished. "Sure."

Meg reached for her overly-sweet coffee as Haley drew him away, her eyes traveling down his slim build in appreciation as they stood in the threshold to the mall. It had grown obvious that Haley and he were not a couple and never would be. He liked her new look. And best of all, he wasn't so interested in Meg that he set off her warning flags.

Meg's eyes dropped to the necklace as she fingered it, feeling the difference between it to her mom's necklace. *At least, not much*, she thought, letting it fall to press into her with a comfortable weight. It looked odd with her mother's necklace, and she finagled the clasp, feeling somehow unburdened when the cool silver slipped from her. "Just until I get home and put you away properly," she promised as she consigned the bejeweled palette to her purse.

Smile fading, she eyed her reflection as she waited for their return, hardly able to see herself under the new style. The faint unease that Haley had been keeping at bay began to rise again. She looked so nice. Nothing like herself. This was what she wanted, but she increasingly felt as if she was a leaf being swirled down a fast river.

Maybe Austin is right, she thought, fingering the stone again. Maybe she should slow down.

But she was very sure she didn't want to go back to her apartment alone. Christopher might still be out there, and he was...troubled. Very troubled, the kind of troubled that tended to spill over and make other people troubled. She didn't like that he had been a client, and then patient, of Dr. Jillium's. That Dr. Jillium had broken the doctor/patient privilege to make sure Meg wasn't lying about the side effects didn't make her feel any better.

Meg's gaze dropped to her purse, her ignored diary still sitting in it like a guilty secret. Maybe she should call Austin and apologize. He was only concerned about her, and apparently, the danger in a bad reaction was significant if Christopher was any indication. Austin had been so good to her, understanding even when she'd been at her lowest point, unable to leave the apartment for a week last Christmas, making sure she ate and even washing her hair for her when it seemed like a mountain.

Her gaze rose to Rorry and Haley standing against the backdrop of the busy shoppers. Haley's hands moved expressively, and a feathering of anxiety brushed against her. Meg looked at the time, relief a warm blanket as she realized she could take another pill. She needed to talk to Austin, yes, but there was no way she could cancel on Haley tonight. Not after Haley had gone to so much trouble in helping her pick out a new dress, and making reservations at Swanks.

New jewelry, she thought wryly as the stone swung when she bent to get her purse and dug about until she found her meds. The *click-click* of the top coming off was familiar, and she hid the rattle of the pills in case Haley looked over. She took one, washing it down with the sweet coffee before dropping the vial back in her purse and edging the diary to cover it. Exhaling, Meg leaned back in her chair, to study her reflection. The stone was warm against her, but the chain was cold, like her curls, and she liked how it felt against her.

Sipping her coffee, she waited for Haley to come back.

Eleven

A hazy warmth rose from the lily-pad covered water, green with life and placid with contentment. The lake lay pressed under the heady afternoon sun, fractured by the slow trickle of water from Haley's oars as she lifted them one final time and stowed them within the rented rowboat. Meg sighed happily, the comfortable lassitude soaking into her until the stress of yesterday's whirlwind had been expunged to leave only the good parts. Fingers shifting her stone pendant back and forth along the gold chain, she felt as if she never wanted anything other than this forever.

"Meg, could you hand me a napkin?" Haley asked. Her tan face was scrunched up in an annoyed distress as she stared at a spider that had crawled out from under the gunwales.

Immediately Meg sat up, startling as the nearby frogs into a scattering of water and motion. The frogs were everywhere.

Kim Harrison

Their singing was unusual this late in the spring, but it only added to the surreal feel to the morning. The harsh slide and clatter of the cooler's plastic lid seemed fake compared to the utter submersion of water, frogs, and moist heat.

Winter seemed to puddle about her fingers as Meg pushed aside the tray of sushi and slushy lemonades to find a condensation-wet napkin. Her back ached pleasantly as she stretched to hand it to Haley, and the woman took it, looking posh in her white sundress and hat as she squished the unfortunate arachnid coming out from a crack for some sun.

My hero, Meg thought dryly as Haley surveyed the rest of the two-seater rowboat for any other spiders before balling the napkin up and dropping it on the algae-stained floorboards.

Haley settled back, and slowly the peace of the day exerted itself again. Meg had slept late, falling asleep quickly and never waking up even once, exhausted by yesterday's shopping capped off by an extravagant salad and two glasses of wine at Swanks. She barely remembered the evening apart from how everyone had treated her with a gratifying respect and deference. Even the walk home was sketchy, with only the memory of laughing at something Haley had said to tell her they had done it…something to do with the empty street and chickens.

She'd woken to the soft sounds of Haley making coffee to find that though Rorry was gone, it was obvious that he'd been there; there was a pile of bags in the corner from their shopping. Meg and Haley had eaten breakfast on the open-aired balcony, and it was so pleasant that Meg actually enjoyed the overly sweet coffee that Haley had made for her. Even using Haley's cinnamon toothpaste instead of her usual mint didn't seem so bad.

It had been Haley herself who had quashed the idea of another shopping day, instead asking Meg what she wanted to do. Boating on the quad's recreational pond/drainage area had been a stammering, hesitant suggestion, but Meg was exhausted. To her surprise, Haley had fixated on the introverted activity with the intensity of a bull terrier on a rat, arranging an upscale picnic basket to be picked up at the local grocery and calling in a reservation at the boat rental. "A Meg day!" the woman had said brightly before finding a second sundress for Meg among her clothes and pronouncing it perfect.

No people, no stress, a Meg day, Meg mused, feeling grateful as she trailed a fingertip into the lake while they slowly lost momentum. They weren't the only two out here among the frogs and lilies, but they were the best dressed, for sure.

Her new waves were a cool brush of sensation on her neck, and she felt pretty in Haley's borrowed dress, the yellow and red reflecting the strong light. She squinted at Haley from under her new white hat, bought off a dusty rack at the boathouse. Haley had an even wider-brimmed hat, and she looked amazingly together as she sat at the stern of the boat and soaked up the sun. It was lazy and serene, hot and sleepy, beautiful with the frogs everywhere as they bumped about the water lilies.

Smiling, Meg shifted her attention to the other boaters. Most were puttering about in the middle of the small lake, lazing about as they were, hands trailing in the water to cool themselves. It looked like a painting, and Meg's artistic soul woke, having been stunned to a shocked silence by yesterday's madcap, extroverted bonanza.

"Gotcha," Haley said, a delicate, sandaled foot shifting to rub out another spider.

A painting of spider eradication, Meg thought, musing that though Van Gogh never put spiders in his paintings, she would. She could call it Spider Lake.

Smiling privately, Meg sat up and took her lemon slushy out of the cooler, leaving Haley's there when the woman shook her head. She was getting used to the absolute tartness that Haley liked in almost everything she ate, and she was glad now that she hadn't told Haley that she didn't like lemonade. The afternoon was so perfect. Why ruin it with the want of a Dr. Pepper?

Happy, Meg trailed a hand in the cool water, trying to find the impetus to get her phone from her purse and take a picture. She'd like to paint this so she'd never forget it. She'd like to paint this while sitting in the sun at Haley's apartment.

Perfunctory Af**fection**

"What a fabulous idea this was," Haley said, her attention on the moth she'd just flicked off the gunwale and into the water, but there wasn't a hint of sarcasm, and Meg felt a flush of relief. "I'm always so busy that I forget to take the time to slow down. Thank you for this. It's just what I needed."

"I'm glad you think so," Meg said hesitantly. "I wasn't sure you would like it. I was afraid you were only doing it because I wanted to." Haley's eyebrows went high, and Meg rushed to add, "The busier it is, the more you come alive. I thought you'd hate coming out here."

"Oh!" Haley shrugged, her attention going to her white sandals, pristine on the green, softly damp bottom of the boat. "Well, a lot of what you saw yesterday was me try-ing to get settled as fast as possible. Now I can relax. And this is wonderful." Sighing, Haley looked out across the lake toward the campus, busy now that it was after noon. "Being out here, watching the world from a quiet point reminds me of home. Maybe that's why I don't let myself slow down." Haley met Meg's eyes. "I'd miss it too much. I think Rorry misses it more than me, but he's younger. Feels everything more deeply."

A thrill of angst went through Meg. She'd been so bold yesterday, agreeing to stay over when she hardly knew them. But that was something she wanted to change. Stirring her lemon slushy, she feigned disinterest. "When is Rorry coming back?"

Kim Harrison

Haley's smile was tinged with a fond anticipation. "Not sure," she said as she opened the cooler and took out her own slushy. "Sometimes it takes a while to talk to everyone. Settle on an agreement, and the, ah, commute isn't always reliable." Her eyes flicked to Meg's. "After a year of being gone, I expect that Rorry won't be that eager to get his ducks in a row and get back here."

"He misses it, huh?" Meg said, remembering how his eyes had lit up when he described his home of mountains and ocean.

Haley nodded. "But this here? Out here on the water, with no one but a few friends to enjoy it with? This comes surprisingly close." Haley's eyes went distant on the shore. "Surprisingly," she almost whispered.

"Tell me?" Meg said, and Haley's focus sharpened on her. Thinking she'd done something wrong, Meg stiffened, but then Haley's attention rose from the necklace Rorry had given her to go distant and dreamy on the weedy, rough side of the pond again.

"The night is alive with parties," she said, her voice seeming to be soaked up by the heat and lilies. "Especially in the summer when the wide doors are pushed back and the night is allowed to come in. There's music and dancing. All kinds. No one thinks it odd when you steal away to avoid the gossip, and no one puts you on the gossip list for doing so. My father has an expansive garden that runs down to a pond like this. I spent much of my childhood rescuing the frogs that had come up to the house looking for the moths that gathered at the lights, not knowing that they would dry out and die." Haley's attention returned to Meg. "I always thought it odd. They strove so hard to reach the very thing that would kill them. But that is the way of things. That I tried to rescue them was one of the reasons I was encouraged to become what I am."

Meg nodded, not knowing what else to do. "Teach language arts?" she finally hazarded, and Haley laughed.

"God, no. That's what I *do*, not what I *am*. No one wants to leave Perfection. I have a knack for it. And we do need resources, things we can't do or make on our own. Me being here helps rectify that and ensure that things at home go on the way they should."

Still not understanding, Meg sipped her lemonade, feeling it cold all the way down.

"But I miss it," Haley said, looking more wistful than Meg had ever seen. "The ocean current keeps us warm all year, and the skies at night are breathtaking, mirrored on the glassy water when conditions are right so it's as if you are sailing through stars. The buildings are all made from the local stone, and they almost glow at night. We have a gardener who paints with plants, and his canvas is always changing with the seasons." Haley went still. "The iris would be blooming now. They are amazing against the pillars and fountains."

"It sounds beautiful," Meg said, thinking her voice seemed coarse after Haley's pure description. "You should go home your next vacation day."

Haley's distant gaze came back, an uncomfortable pinch to her eyes. "I get home quite often, actually, but you know. Work. I can't do it from there." Haley laughed ruefully, but her shoulders were slumped, and for the first time, she looked depressed.

Meg nodded, not knowing how to react. Perfection sounded utterly pastoral. They'd need an incoming source of money from their young people, and a teacher, especially a language arts teacher, would require a big university to get the students. Haley and Rorry were probably supporting not just themselves, but their families as well.

Looking at Haley, Meg was suddenly struck at her flawless beauty, even when unhappy and missing her home. Meg looked down at her gold necklace and borrowed dress, even her haircut and painted nails a gift from Haley. Austin's ring on her pinky looked coarse next to her perfect nails, making Meg feel as if she was faking what Haley and Rorry truly were. "Maybe next time you go home, I can come with you," Meg said hesitantly. "I'd love to see your dad's garden."

Haley's smile was wan. "Maybe."

The brush-off in her one-word answer, made her feel as if she wasn't good enough to bring home. Shoving the ugly feeling away, Meg searched out her phone. "You mind if I take a few pictures? I need a prompt for class tomorrow."

"No. Go right ahead." Haley was all smiles again, but a hint of her mood lingered. "Send me the best one. I'll share it with Rorry. He thinks all I do is work and shop."

Thinking that she was blowing it, Meg snuck a pill under the excuse of getting her phone. The vial had slid under her diary, and again she promised herself that tonight she'd write down when she'd been taking her pills.

This is good, she thought, relaxing as she began to catalog the afternoon in a series of shots, beginning with a close-up of the rowboat's thole before moving on to a frog on a lily pad, and then pulling back to a wider angle showing boats and the campus behind them. She could use her method to fragment the boat, or maybe the lily. Haley, reclining in the sun, could be reduced to a few curving lines. *Yes, this might work,* she thought, warming to the task. If her technique worked on familiar objects, it would shine if she could translate it to subjects that were already uncertain.

The hum of her phone in her hand shocked through her, and Meg almost dropped it. Gasping, she looked up, laughing at herself as she realized she'd been so engrossed that she'd forgotten Haley was even there. But her amusement ground to dust when she saw who was calling.

"Austin?" Haley guessed at Meg's sour expression.

"Yep." Meg looked at the picture of Austin wearing a silly hat and sipping a peppermint milkshake. "Do you mind if I take this?" she asked, embarrassed. "If I don't, he's going to keep calling." Meg's attention went to the distant boathouse, relieved to see he wasn't standing at the end of the dock, watching her.

"Sure, I don't mind." Haley unshipped the oars, and Meg hit the accept key when Haley's first strong pull angled them back into the shade that hung about the edges.

Head down, Meg put the phone to her ear. "Hi, Austin. I told you I'd call you Monday. I'm out with Haley right now," she said tightly, the peace of the day shattered.

"Please don't hang up." Austin sounded anxious, and Meg rolled her eyes to make Haley smile. "I made a mistake, and I'm so sorry. I never should have moved out."

He's missing me? she thought, a flash of vindication warming her as they slipped into the shade. "No, you shouldn't have, but you did."

"Look. I want to talk to you about moving back in," he said, and alarm slid through her, unexpected and potent. "Can we have lunch?" he rushed. "Just the two of us. Wherever you want. We could have milkshakes at putt-putt, or coffee, or maybe we could take a drive out to Manchester and hit that art studio you love. It won't be busy on a day this nice."

He wanted her to go back to the way she'd been, and her shoulders rose as she tried to wall off the fear. Her familiar haunts seemed tame after last night's dinner at Swanks, a part of her she wanted to leave behind. "I told you, I'm out with Haley. I've already got lunch plans," she said, her downed gaze alighting on the cooler of sushi. "Austin, I need some space while I find myself. You calling every day isn't exactly giving me the time I need."

"That's just it," he said, the concern in his voice making her feel defensive. "I'm worried about you, Meg. I know it's what you want, but just let me see you to make sure you're okay. Coffee, maybe. Five minutes to be sure you're happy. That's all I ask."

But five minutes might be enough to drag her back down to what she had been trying to escape for three years. Now that she was almost there, she would not lose focus. She would not go back to anything less.

"I'm fine," she said, believing it to her core. "I'm happy." *I am happy*, she thought in surprise. *I'm happy without him.*

"I'm sure you are," Austin said. "But I need to see it—"

"I'm hanging up now," Meg said, not liking that he made it sound as if he thought her happiness was a delusion. "Please don't call me again. I love you, Austin, but I need some time to think."

"Meg."

Meg jumped when Haley reached across the boat and grabbed the phone right out of her hand. "Meg and I are moving to Rio to become strippers. Bye, bye!" Color high,

Haley hung up. "That should do it," she said, putting the phone into Meg's slack grasp.

For three heartbeats, Meg stared at her, then she began to laugh. Haley joined her, and their twined voices skipped across the lily pads and out to the center of the lake. Slowly Meg's smile faded, but the good feeling lingered like a sunbeam.

What am I doing here? she wondered. Haley was so perfect, so posh. And she was so messed up.

"Everything okay?" Haley said as she took her hat off to fan the heat away. Her golden hair was a mess under it, and even that made her look attractive.

The last of Meg's smile vanished. She didn't want to ruin it by talking about a bad boyfriend, but Haley had heard half the conversation. "Yes and no," she hedged. "Austin wants to talk to me. Make sure I can survive without him. He wants to move back in, and honestly, I don't have a legal right to stop him. It's his name on the lease."

"Mmmm." Haley pursed her lips. "You know...you're more than welcome to stay with Rorry and me for a while."

Meg's head jerked up, twin feelings of angst and anticipation bringing her shoulders tight. "I wouldn't want to impose."

But Haley only smiled wider. "Impose? Are you kidding? Rorry won't mind, and I know I don't. He might even take the couch so you can have that second bedroom. It's just until you get your own place. Right?" she soothed. "We can go over this afternoon and get your things. Pull them out before Austin finds out what's going on." Haley's expression shifted. "Unless you don't want to."

"I'd love to." Meg's pulse hammered, but she'd say just about anything to get that disappointed look off Haley's face. "Thank you. Thank you so much. But you don't have to come over. I don't have that much I want to bring, and I don't want you there if I run into Austin. I can do it myself. I want to. I should."

Haley seemed to hesitate. "Are you sure? I don't mind. And me being there might help in case Austin gets ugly."

But Meg shook her head, knowing that Austin would more likely sit there in shock, then get angry, if he came home and found her packing. What really scared her was Haley seeing her dark existence. "Positive," she said, pulse fast as she remembered Haley's abhorrence to carrying a few bags back from the mall. There was no way she was going to ask Haley to help her sort through her stuff for the parts she wanted to keep, the things that wouldn't ruin it all. "Do you want a dragon roll?" she asked, trying to change the subject.

"Oh, yes please." Haley resettled herself, and the boat drifted back into the sun as Meg handed her one on a napkin. She desperately wanted to find the earlier perfection of the afternoon, but Austin had spoiled it.

Twelve

Meg cautiously fitted the key to her apartment, trying to make it soundless as it turned. Her car was in the lot, but that didn't mean he wasn't here. He shouldn't be. He said he was going to move out. Austin, though, had been acting erratically lately.

Cracking the door, she listened at the silence for a moment before going in. Exhaling, Meg took in the dark shadows. Everything was the way she'd left it. The drapes were pulled mostly shut, and there was a thickness in the air she didn't remember but which felt familiar. "I hate this place," she whispered as she set her purse on the counter between the living room and the kitchen.

She'd been gone only a day, but it felt longer, and she couldn't help but compare her apartment to the bright openness of Haley's. The cheerful woman was there right now, unpacking the pillows, sheers, and rugs that they'd picked out together, deciding where they went, making the perfect apartment. Looking over the brown carpet, tan walls, and oversized TV that served as the living room's focal point, Meg realized there was nothing she wanted to bring. The only thing that had any meaning were her paintings. Everything else would be a dark stain of imperfection in the Spartan grace that Haley was making.

"The tree might be okay, though," she said softly as she walked to her working easel. The overhead light was off, and she took the shadowed canvas to the window overlooking the parking lot, angling it into the meager light. The fractured tree seemed to glow, and she decided she'd bring it if only because Haley had liked it. It was what had brought them together, she realized. Maybe she should give it to her as a thank-you.

Setting the canvas on the kitchen counter to take, Meg went back for her pigments, brushes, and cleaning supplies. They made a small pile beside her picture, and an unexpected feeling of excitement took her as she saw a new beginning there. She was going to do this. She was going to move out.

Purse in hand, Meg strode into the bedroom. Ignoring the unmade double bed and the dull brown comforter, she grabbed a handful of bras and panties from the dresser. Out. She needed to get what she needed and get out.

Perfunctory **Af**fection

Pulse fast, she flung open the door to her closet, knowing exactly what she'd find. Her shoulders slumped as she absently shoved her underthings into her purse, wincing at the grandma cut of her nightgown even as she wadded it up and dropped it in. As homely as it was, she wasn't going to sleep in one of Haley's spare nightgowns a second time.

With that thought in mind, she grabbed a pair of jeans and three of her most colorful, outlandish tops. Brow furrowed, she took the dress that she'd worn at her last show, the long black shift looking out of place in the faded closet light. And then, feeling as if it was the last tie to a past she didn't want, she dropped it on the floor.

It was too flamboyant for day-to-day, and too drab for a night out. Haley would roll her eyes and pat her on the head.

Purse over her shoulder, Meg went into the bathroom. Her reflected motion caught her eye, and she stopped, startled. Slowly pulling herself straight, Meg touched her curls. A smile spread across her face, and she ran a hand down her slim waist, liking how Haley's sun dress made her look both young and smart all at the same time. Classy. Something everyone might want to be.

Her dark hair glistened against her, and her face was pink from having gotten too much sun. Her eyes seemed like dark, soulful pits, and a faint smile ruined her studious expression. Rorry's necklace glinted about her neck, catching the light and sending it to all corners of the plastic shower-curtained, bar-soap-scummed, brown-toweled, flat-rugged bathroom.

"I can't do dull anymore," she whispered, then dropped down to hunt under the counter for her hairbrush, her seldom-used makeup bag and an even less-used curling iron. They clattered onto the brown Formica counter, sounding like a death-rattle. Her toothbrush went with them, but she left her toothpaste, not wanting Haley to smell mint on her breath.

She jammed it all in her purse, the need to be done and gone hesitating as she found her mother's necklace. Her brow furrowed as she took it out, carefully untangling it and holding it up to the light. The colorful jewels that had once seemed so brilliant now looked common. She imagined wearing it in front of Haley's father, seeing his smile that held his low opinion. Suddenly the need to leave everything behind that reminded her of her depression was almost overwhelming.

"Sorry, Mom," she whispered as she carefully draped it across the bathroom counter. "I have to let you go or I'll never get better."

Somehow her purse seemed lighter as she took it up and walked out into the living room, stopping stock-still when she saw Austin in the kitchen, a horrified expression on his face as he brought his attention up from her canvas and paint supplies.

Perfunctory **Af**fection

"What are you doing?" he asked, his relief shifting to anger as he saw her overstuffed purse with her curling iron poking out.

"Moving out." Pulse fast, she hitched her purse up higher on her shoulder. "I'm going to stay with Haley for a few days until I find my own place."

Austin's expression blanked. "This is your place."

"This is not my place," Meg said, her anger rising. "It's your place. It's you." She gestured at nothing. "Everywhere it's you. None of this is me! It's all dark walls and brown carpet and your movies and games. There is no sun in here, and I hate it!"

"So we'll change it." Austin came out from behind the counter, and Meg's lips pressed into a hard line. "We can pick out a cute basket at the mall for me to hide my console and games in. Maybe get some new furniture. Paint the walls. New drapes. Whatever you want," he said. "You're the one who wanted to live here. You think I like living in this dark cave?"

"I think you like *me* living in a dark cave," Meg said, ignoring that she'd been the one to pick out their place. "I think *you* need someone to save, so you keep me down where you can rescue me Monday through Friday, and twice on Sunday."

"Hey!" Austin barked angrily, but she'd stepped forward, her words rushing to run over his protest.

"I don't need saving anymore," she said as she dug through her purse to find her key. "You can have the place. Do what you want." Taking the key off the ring, she dropped it on the floor and started to her canvas and paints.

"That's not true," Austin said, and she jerked to a halt when he lurched to get in front of her. "Why are you doing this?" he pleaded.

"Because you won't leave me alone!" she shouted, but instead of yelling back at her, he shook his head, his brow furrowed.

"Meg, something is wrong. We need to talk to Dr. Jillium. Today."

A cold chill took her, and she backed up a step. "I know the symptoms of a bad reaction and I'm not showing any of them," she said as she backed up another. "Everything tastes normal. I'm not having stranger anxiety, and nothing is giving me a rash. I'm even sleeping better. I haven't had even one nightmare. I'm fine."

"You are not fine." Frustrated, Austin gestured at her. "Look at you. I hardly recognize you. Where did you get that dress?"

Meg licked her lips. "It's Haley's," she said. "She's letting me borrow it."

"You sure it's not from that shopping spree that came in over your card yesterday?" Austin said dryly. "It set off your fraud protection alert."

Perfunctory Af**fection**

Anger trickled through Meg. She couldn't win for losing. "I bought a pair of sandals," she said. "It was Dr. Jillium's homework to get out and go shopping, and now you're mad at me for that? Haley was the one buying the store out. And what's the problem? You like the way I looked before?" Angry, she pointed at the bedroom. "Fine. Everything of mine is still in the closet. You can dress up a doll, prop her in the chair, and get the same result."

"That's not what I'm saying," Austin said, but he hadn't moved from the door, and she felt trapped, even if his eyes had gone soft and unsure. "You look great, but this is too much too fast. Out all night. Shopping during the busy hours. I haven't seen you for days it seems."

"It's what normal people do, Austin," she said bitterly, not liking herself for having been so dysfunctional.

"Yes, I know." His voice was softer, appeasing, and he moved from the door a step closer to her. "But if I learned anything about medication these past few years, I learned that what goes up comes down, and you are up. You're up too high for me to catch you when you fall."

She stiffened, not liking his idea that everything she had achieved was all chemically induced. "I'm not going to fall," she said. "And I don't want you to catch me. You know what? We're done." Dropping her purse on the couch, she began to twist her pinky ring off.

"Wait. Meg." Austin backed up, a hand raised in protest. "Don't. Just don't. Please. If you won't talk to me, talk to Dr. Jillium. I think you're having a bad reaction."

Meg wrestled with the pinky ring. "For the first time in three years, I don't need you," she said, finger hurting as she finally raked it over her knuckle. "I think you're the one who is having a bad reaction." She exhaled, triumphant as she threw it at him. Austin fumbled for it, his damaged fingers obvious as he tried to keep it from hitting the floor.

"Don't call or text me anymore. Got it?" she said, knees watery, but it was because she was mad, not afraid. "And if you even think about talking to Dr. Jillium, I'll… I'll…" Her words trailed off. There was nothing she could say that she was sure she was brave enough to carry out.

"Meg—"

He reached for her, and she jerked out of his reach. "Leave me alone!" she shouted, startled when her voice filled the dark room. "I'm not going to let you drag me back to what I was!"

"I'm not trying to," he pleaded, her ring held in a tight fist. "I just want to help. Something isn't right, and you aren't listening!"

"You're the one not listening!" she exclaimed as she picked up her purse. "I like who I am, and I'm sorry, but it doesn't include you anymore. You're right. You and Dr. Jillium were right. You are a crutch, and I have to let you go. Goodbye, Austin."

Jaw clenched, she went to the kitchen and got her canvas. Furious, she stuffed the pigments into her purse. Brushes in a tight fist, she headed for the door.

"Meg," he said, reaching for her again.

"Let go!" she shouted as his two good fingers pinched her arm, and in almost a panic, she shoved him away.

Austin backpedaled, arms wheeling as he fell into the couch. For a second, he stared up at her, and it was not clear who was more surprised. Slowly Austin got to his feet, his hands in his pockets as he stood and glowered at her. "You aren't yourself," he said, clearly angry. "When and if you are, I'll be here."

Meg lifted her chin. "I'm not coming back." Wedging her brushes into her already too-full purse, she stomped to the door and walked out, slamming the door behind her.

The noise made her jump, and not believing what she'd done, she hustled down the stairs, stumbling out into the bright afternoon sun. It hit her like a wall, and she took a deep breath, shaking off the ugliness behind her.

Just as well, she thought as she made her way to the sidewalk. If she hadn't ended everything right then, it would have festered. And at least now she'd know exactly what she and Dr. Jillium *wouldn't* be talking about tomorrow.

"Hey! Can you tell they aren't real yet?" a ragged voice yelled, and Meg stopped short, her canvas held tight as she saw Christopher and his dog across the street.

Kim Harrison

Son of a bitch.... Options fell through Meg's thoughts, unrecognized as her gut demanded that she run from him, the darkest threat to her new self. A surge of anger swirled forth, smothering it. Jaw clenched, she pushed her fear aside. She didn't want to be that person. She wouldn't.

"Go away!" she shouted, and the car passing between them slowed, its driver curious. "You hear me?" she added as she started across the street, almost oblivious to the oncoming traffic. "Go away! Get out of here! Leave me alone!"

That dog of his was barking wildly, and looking panicked, Christopher scooped it up and fled, the ragged hems of his pants flapping.

Shocked, Meg stopped in the middle of the street and watched him run away. An oncoming car braked fast, tires squealing. The sound ripped through her, and for a second, she couldn't move, frozen by the memory of hitting that tree three years ago, the sudden jerk, the clean sensation of pain pushing whatever argument they'd been having into oblivion. *Austin had been with me.*

"Get the hell out of the road!" the man shouted, and red-faced, she hurried to the curb. The car accelerated with a tight squeal of tires, and she warmed at his added, "Stupid woman!" Meg risked a look back, even more embarrassed when she realized that Austin had seen it all, his unmoving figure standing beside the mailboxes. His hands were still in his pockets, and his lips were pressed into a tight line. Saying nothing, he pushed into motion and jogged unevenly after Christopher.

Whatever, she thought as she hoisted her canvas higher up her hip and moved faster. Everything would be fine as soon as she got back to Haley. No, everything would be perfect.

Thirteen

Meg tripped on the uneven sidewalk, her grip on the canvas tightening and her overloaded purse threatening to spill. Her embarrassment at yelling at Christopher had faded, leaving only a shocked amazement that she'd dumped Austin. Three years, and she was walking away to move in with someone she barely knew. *Change is hard, or everyone would do it*, she thought, echoing one of Dr. Jillium's favorite sayings. *But exciting when you're the one in control*, she added silently.

Her entire body felt light, and it seemed as if her feet barely touched the sidewalk as she came to a halt and hit the button for the crosswalk, still riding the high. She wasn't helpless. She could stand on her own.

It was busier down here. University Dregs, the local coffee/WiFi hangout, was across the street, and the rich scent of coffee rolled out onto the sidewalk to entice her in.

Almost she wished she had the time, but Haley was waiting for her, and there was an entire apartment to decorate.

"You shouldn't have left your apartment. It makes it easier for them to strip your identity," a masculine voice said from behind her. Meg spun, her lips parting when she saw Christopher, his eyes holding a wary regret. His dog was gone, and she looked over his shoulder for Austin.

"Go away," she said, feeling trapped between him and the traffic. "I swear, if you don't leave me alone, I'm going to call the cops." She set her canvas on the sidewalk, fumbling to find her phone in her purse. "Where's Austin? Did he put you up to this? How much is he paying you to harass me?"

"Who?" Christopher saw the phone in her hand, and he backed up, hand raised. "No one is paying me anything," he said. "I'm trying to help you, and you're not listening. Leaving your apartment is making it easy for them, but it's not too late, even if you can see them. I can help. Will you just listen to me for one blessed moment?"

He was sounding almost coherent, and a chill dropped down Meg's spine when he caught sight of her painted canvas and his expression shifted to one of horror. "That's why they want you," he whispered, staring at it as if it was a snake. "Oh, God. That's why. They can't do it, any of it, so they find people who can, and they lure them away. But it's slavery. They won't ever let you come back. You can never do enough to please them."

Perfunctory **Af**fection

Meg pressed into the street post, torn between running to the coffee shop or making a break for Haley's place. But then he'd know where she was staying, and so she didn't move, trapped between him and the traffic. *Better humor him,* she thought, as she texted 911 to Daniel. "Can't do what?" she asked, sending her location to him as well.

"Create." Christopher's erratic attention darted over the passing cars. "They can't create anything; art, music, an exceptional dinner. Creation is messy and ugly, an imperfect mix of trial and failure. That's why they want you," he said, and Meg clutched her phone to her middle, feeling it vibrate as Daniel texted he was on his way.

"It's your imperfections that draw them," Christopher implored as he looked at her canvas again, and it was as if seeing it triggered an entirely new set of mannerisms, his new, large-word vocabulary at odds with his torn, stained clothes. "The more innovative we are, the more we attract them, and the more they want us, and the more they hate us. Because we can do what they can't. They crave the result, but despise the process."

My God, this guy is really messed up, she thought, wondering what he'd been before he lost his marbles.

"Dr. Jillium knows about them," he said as he eyed her. "I told her," he added, and Meg wondered if "they" were the ones that he kept asking if she could see. "That's why she tucked me away in that mental hospital. She thinks they're a side effect of the Fitrecepon, but the only side effect is that it lets us see them. Oh, God! I was so stupid."

Hallucinations, she thought, scared. Dr. Jillium said they were possible. She backed up when he took a step closer, her heels on the curb. *Hurry up, Daniel…*

"They've been here all the time," Christopher said, and the stink of too long without a shower pricked at her nose when he leaned in, whispering. "It's the Fitrecepon. It lets you see them. Makes them real. Stop taking the pills. It's not too late. She thinks I'm schizophrenic and imagining them, but they're real. They are real, I tell you!" he shouted, and she backed up, right into the street. "Don't let her tell you they aren't!"

"Let go!" she cried out when he grabbed her arm and jerked her back onto the sidewalk and out of the path of an oncoming car.

Her pulse hammered as she twisted away, but she didn't run, desperate for Daniel to show up. The fractured pendant that Rorry had given her swung free, and Chris gasped as he saw it.

"Don't go with them," he said as he backed up, one hand stuffed behind his tattered shirt as if he'd burned his fingers. "Don't do it," he almost hissed, eyes darting. "You aren't one of them. They only make you think you are. If you were, they wouldn't want you. I escaped, but they know how I did it and it will be harder to do twice."

Meg held the stone, unable to look away from his wild, spittle-flying demands. Behind her, the light changed. Grabbing her canvas, she crossed the street. She could hear Chris following. If she went in, Daniel might not find her, so she spun to put her back to the bike stand to wait. *Why doesn't he go away!*

"You have to kill them," he whispered, and she jerked when he brandished the hand he'd been hiding. She stared, transfixed, at his truncated ring finger. *Did he chop it off?* she wondered. "It's the only way," he said, voice hushed. "I'll help you, but you have to get rid of that stone. Now. They can track you through it. It's a slave collar."

He reached for her. Panicked, she shoved him away. "Get off!" she shouted, and he fell into the coffee shop's planter. Annoyed, as he gathered himself to rise. But then he hesitated, his attention drawn to a car screeching to a halt in the nearby parking lot.

It was Daniel, and relief swept her as the lanky man bolted out of the car.

"You stupid fool." Chris's eyes pinched in annoyance, and then he turned and fled.

"That way!" Meg shouted when Daniel ran to her instead of following Chris. "He went that way!"

"Stay here. I want to talk to you," Daniel said, and she froze, shocked at the smooth clink of handcuffs as he locked her to the bike rack.

"Hey!" she exclaimed, as he took off after Chris. "What are you doing?"

"I'll be right back!" he called over his shoulder, and then he turned a corner and was gone.

"Son of a biscuit," she swore mildly, then looked up, shifting to hide the cuffs and smile at the couple going into the shop. The sun was hot, and she managed to get her phone out, ticked as she called Dr. Jillium. It wasn't as if she could call Austin. Besides, she wanted to ask her if Chris had really been a patient of hers…and how he managed to land in a psych ward after taking Fitrecepon.

Jaw clenched, Meg waited as the phone hummed. The notarized medical waivers were starting to make a lot more sense. Sure, she had warned Meg about the side effects, but landing in a mental hospital with imaginary friends hadn't been one of them. *Or had it?*

Meg's shoulders slumped when Dr. Jillium finally picked up. "Meg!" the woman exclaimed brightly, and then after an awkward hesitation, "How's your weekend going?"

"Peachy." Her back to the store, Meg hid that she was cuffed from the older man going in. "A detective just locked me to a bike rack outside of University Dregs so he could chase down one of your former patients."

"Uh, what?" the woman asked, and Meg's lips pressed at the guilt in her voice.

"Daniel Hun?" Meg questioned, feeling vindicated. She had a right to be upset. "He's chasing Christopher."

"Oh, my God. Chris? Meg, are you okay?" Dr. Jillium blurted, and Meg stifled a shudder.

"What's wrong with him?" Meg asked, the sun unable to warm her. "Is it the Fitrecepon? What did you put me on?"

Dr. Jillium sighed. Meg could hear it clear through the connection. "I told you there were occasional complications. Chris has problems, but none of them stem from Fitrecepon. I'm at my office. I can be there in just a few minutes."

"That would be nice," Meg said sourly, but Dr. Jillium had already hung up. Meg awkwardly wrangled her phone closed and stuffed it in a pocket. Looking up, she smiled weakly at the couple coming out, hoping none of her students saw her leaning with a forced casualness against the bike rack as if waiting for a John. She scanned the sidewalk for Dr. Jillium, wondering if it would take a cop to get the cuffs off or if Dr. Jillium had a special skill set that Meg wasn't aware of.

But Meg pulled herself straight, her fake smile failing when Daniel showed up first, alone, and looking hot in his black suit and tie. "Sorry," he said when he got close enough. "I didn't think you'd wait, and I wanted to talk to you."

Ticked, she stepped aside so he could undo the cuff. His shadow blanketed her wrist, and she tugged free, watching him fold the cuffs up and tuck them in a back belt holster with a clinking, practiced motion. "I'm the one that called you, remember?" she said. "Am I under arrest?"

Daniel ran a quick hand over his mouth to hide his smile. "No. You want a coffee? It's the least I can do for cuffing you to a bike rack. We can play information," he added when she picked up her things in a huff. "I tell you stuff, and you tell me stuff."

Meg's eyes narrowed, but information sounded like a pleasant change. "Fine," she said, rubbing her wrist as if she could still feel the hard steel there. "But I get the first question." Pushing past him, she went in and dropped her canvas and purse at the small table by the window that she and Austin always used. There was no one waiting in line, and she ordered one of Haley's sugar bombs instead of her typical black coffee. Daniel ordered an iced coffee, his hands in his pockets and his focus distant on the menu as he rocked back and forth on his heels. The baristas were too close to ask him anything, and so they waited until their drinks came up.

She was still mad when they went to sit down, and Meg took her usual spot in the sun. There was a spider spinning a web outside the window, and she stifled the urge to go out and crush it. They were bad this year, God knew why. "Me first," she said, and Daniel's obvious bliss in the cold drink vanished. "Is he dangerous?"

Perfunctory **Af**fection

The young man leaned back, his suit giving him a sly-businessman-like mien as he stirred the ice with his straw. "Chris? Only if you listen to him. What did he tell you?"

Meg took a slow sip, the coffee so full of sugar it felt like syrup. "Not much," she admitted, eyes down. "He rambled on about being able to see them, whoever 'they' are. That they were real, and that they'd kidnap me unless I helped him kill them."

"Did he say how he'd do it?"

Meg's eyes darted up to his, shocked at the tension he was trying to hide.

The jingle of the door opening drew his attention, and his expression eased into a slight frown.

"Daniel," Dr. Jillium said as she came in, looking casual in her jeans and light top. "You should have called me. I need to know when one of my patients goes on walkabout."

Daniel looked between the two of them, his worry vanishing at Meg's relieved smile. "Dr. Jillium," he said as he stood, shifting a chair to make room for her. "I was just about to do that. I'm glad to see you. You look great."

Brushing past his outstretched hand, Dr. Jillium leaned to peer at Meg. "Are you okay? You don't have to talk to him," she added, lips pressing into a thin line as she gave Daniel a sidelong glance.

"I'm fine now that I'm not locked to a bike rack." Meg eyed them both suspiciously. Daniel was scrubbing a hand across his cleanly shaven face as if embarrassed. "You two know each other?" she asked, but the answer was obvious.

Daniel's smile became strained. "We've done business before."

"Business?" Meg echoed, tucking her purse deeper under her chair. Dr. Jillium had noticed it, and she really didn't want to talk about why her curling iron and hairbrush were poking out of it.

Motion full of grace, Dr. Jillium sat down. "Daniel and I met the first time Chris escaped the hospital. I'm not happy with his techniques to reacquire him. Playing along with a client's delusions in order to entrap them is not morally right."

Daniel's smile widened to crinkle his eyes. "But it is effective. Can I get you a coffee, Doc? I could use your help in building a framework for his probable patterns this go around."

This happens a lot? Meg wondered, becoming more uneasy. Just what had Dr. Jillium given her?

But Dr. Jillium was looking at Meg's cup. "That's not your usual," she said warily, and Meg flushed.

"I'm expanding my palate," she said, then took a sip to prove that she was enjoying it.

Daniel rocked back, turning to the ordering counter. "It was black, wasn't it, Doc? With a little sugar?"

Dr. Jillium nodded, setting her purse on Daniel's chair when he went to stand in the new line, hands in his pockets to look innocuous. But Meg had her doubts.

"Where is your mom's necklace?" she asked, and Meg jerked. "It's not making you itch, is it?"

Eyebrows high, Meg reached for her new one, the smooth feel of it different in her hand. Dr. Jillium saw everything. "No," she said as she spun the cool length of gold to hide the clasp. "I just took it off is all. It was time to start letting go."

"Oh." Dr. Jillium's suspicion seemed to ease as she peered appreciatively at it. "That's beautiful. I don't think I've ever seen that kind of a stone before. Your ring is gone, too."

Lips pressed, Meg looked at her splayed fingers, seeing the pale line of skin where Austin's ring had been. "Ah, yeah," she hedged, fighting back a surge of anger. "It's all part of that letting go thing. Dr. Jillium, who is Christopher?"

Apparently satisfied, Dr. Jillium straightened, her posture perfect as she primly pushed the cinnamon container still at the table to the window. "You know I can't talk about other patients with you," she said cagily.

"That boat sailed yesterday," Meg insisted. "Who is he, and what happened to him?" she asked again, and when Dr. J hesitated, she added, "I'm on the same thing he was. Is? I deserve to know. Especially if he's stalking me."

Kim Harrison

Frowning, Dr. Jillium glanced up at Daniel before scooting her chair closer. Her tightly braided hair glistened as she leaned in, and Meg caught the faint scent of whatever she oiled it with. The first hints of gray were showing, and Meg thought it unfair that it only made her look more professional, more graceful, somehow.

"He was a games specialist," Dr. Jillium said softly. "One of those people who can build an entire world to play in on the internet. Marvelous imagination. He was in the top of his field for a time in creating story lines for new games, and he came to me after he began having difficulty accepting the loss of his son and wife."

Meg nodded. Dr. Jillium specialized in grief-borne issues. It was why she'd gone to her after her mother's death.

"I started him on Fitrecepon to get him back into making life-affirming decisions," Dr. Jillium was saying, her eyes on her clasped hands resting on the table. They were dark in the sun, and gracefully thin and long, and Meg realized only now there was no wedding ring, no nothing.

"It was before we knew the early signs of a bad reaction." Dr. Jillium looked up, the heartache in her eyes surprising Meg. "He was having multiple, paranoid hallucinations before I knew it and could take him off the Fitrecepon. I'm sorry to say that despite several years of therapy, he continues to believe there is a mirror world where he can go and find respite from his pain. He says it's where the fey live, which I would think odd except for his mythology background that he used in formatting his computer worlds. Stories of elves stealing the unwary are not uncommon."

"Take him to a perfect world," Meg said, remembering Christopher saying something about utopia.

Dr. Jillium's tightly clasped hands sprang apart. "He told you?" she asked, their smooth length on the table, and Meg shrugged, embarrassed to have been caught up in someone else's delusions even this lightly. It was like looking in their underwear drawer and comparing brands.

"He, ah, wanted to help me kill them," Meg said, and Dr. Jillium's expression blanked. "Elves?" Meg asked, thinking that Christopher's question of "Can you see them?" suddenly made sense in an odd way. No, she couldn't see them, but that he thought she could gave her the willies.

"He insists that the fey took him there and that he escaped, but the only place he's escaped from is the hospital." Dr. Jillium glanced at Daniel waiting at the pickup counter. "Several times, now. Meg, I'm so sorry," she added, actually giving her hand a quick squeeze. "You shouldn't have gotten caught up in this. I didn't know Chris had escaped again. That he found you is unfortunate. He must have seen you leave my office and is after more Fitrecepon. It was responsible for the hallucinations, so in a way, it would give him a path to escape reality again."

Meg nodded, though Christopher had made it very clear that he didn't want any of the drug. No, he didn't want *her* to take any. Maybe he was planning to go through her trash for them?

"How many pills do you have left?" Dr. Jillium asked, and Meg jerked at a stab of angst. She wouldn't take her off it, would she? "I'm not sure," Meg said faintly, but it wasn't more than a day's worth at this point, and both of them knew it.

"You should have about four or five left," Dr. Jillium said as she flipped through an app on her phone. "I'm not comfortable giving you more than a day's dose at a time until Christopher is found. Would you find it too difficult to stop in every day and pick up a twenty-four-hour supply until he's back in custody?"

Meg fought to hide her relief. "No, that would be fine," she said lightly, and Dr. Jillium smiled.

"Thanks. I know it's a pain, but I'd feel better. I just want what's best for you, and you seem to be responding well to it." Again she glanced at Daniel. "Is that yours, or a student's?" she asked, her attention falling to Meg's canvas.

Meg took a breath of air and held it, not wanting to explain why it was sitting next to her purse. "Ah, mine," she finally said as she showed it to her, and Dr. Jillium took it, carefully handling it by the edges with the palms of her hands.

"It's beautiful." Dr. Jillium tilted it so the strong light made the black lines almost glow. "No wonder your class tripled over winter break. The way you define with only a third of the subject leaving the mind to fill in the rest...I don't think I've ever seen anything like it."

"Haley said the same thing," Meg took it back, modestly setting it out of the way where no one else could see it. "That's why I'm going to give it to her."

"Haley?" Dr. Jillium predictably asked, and Meg smiled, doggedly determined not to bring up having broken up with Austin. Not yet. Tomorrow was soon enough.

"She's my new friend," Meg admitted, thinking it funny a grown woman would be so proud of it. "The one you told me to make? I'm taking your homework very seriously, so new sandals, new friend." *New life*, she thought. "We went to the mall yesterday. Had dinner out at a new place afterward. Her brother gave me the necklace."

Dr. Jillium smiled, her gaze rising from Meg's offered sandaled foot to the necklace. "And Austin?" she prompted.

Meg dropped her eyes. Steeling herself, she forced them to meet Dr. Jillium's. "I think we're done," she said softly as her pulse quickened. "You were right that he was a crutch. He loves me, but he'd rather I stay the way I was. He wants me just well enough to function, but not well enough to be able to stand on my own. He should be seeing you, not me," she said, still not going to tell her she was temporarily moving in with Haley.

"Meg, I'm so proud of you," Dr. Jillium said, her absolutely beaming smile the last thing Meg had expected to see. "This is a very big breakthrough," she added, giving Meg's hand a quick squeeze. "I'm so pleased that you finally see that you don't need Austin to function. Your progress will move forward much faster now."

She doesn't care that I broke up with Austin? Meg thought, confused.

"Coffee!" Daniel sang out as he suddenly appeared behind Dr. Jillium and set a large paper cup beside her. Both women went silent as he sat down, Dr. Jillium taking her first sip as Meg tried to figure this out. Dr. Jillium seemed more than indifferent about her cutting Austin out of her life. She actually seemed pleased. All this time Meg had thought Dr. Jillium wanted her to work things out, make concessions, but it had only been a psychological task to get her to make a positive choice for the right reasons.

Suddenly Meg felt uncomfortable, and she stood up, and gathered her things. "Can I go?" she asked, and the two of them looked blankly at her. "I've told you everything I know, and I've got someone waiting for me."

"Haley?" Dr. Jillium asked, and Meg nodded since it seemed to be the right thing to say.

"I just have one question," Daniel said, his elbows on the table as he leaned over it. "Did Chris tell you where he was going?"

Perfunctory **Af****fection**

Meg hitched her purse higher up on her shoulder, trying to hide it behind her back so Dr. Jillium wouldn't see what was in it. "No. Sorry."

Daniel threw a hand carelessly into the air and slumped back in his chair. "Then I'm done. Unless he contacts you again."

Meg began inching away. "Sure. If you promise not to lock me to a bike rack. Again."

Daniel grinned, looking boyishly attractive, but it only made Dr. Jillium frown. "Don't forget your coffee," Dr. Jillium said, and Meg half crouched to take it, keeping her purse behind her back. "I'll see you tomorrow, Meg, but call me if you see Chris." She hesitated, glancing at Daniel. "Or if anything seems wrong. Okay?"

"Okay. Monday," Meg said, anxious to be back in the sun.

Pace fast, she wove through the tables, looking back once to see Daniel and Dr. Jillium already in a hot argument, their heads close and their body language obvious. Not a flicker of guilt crossed her as she dropped her coffee in the trash and went out onto the sidewalk.

Her eyes darted up and down the busy street, but she found a confident pace once she decided Chris wasn't waiting. Mood easing, she played with the necklace that Rorry had given her, her thoughts on what she and Haley might do today. She felt good when she was with Haley, and right now, that was all that mattered.

Fourteen

t was the breeze that woke Meg, a cool breath of summer sliding into Haley's apartment to find her asleep on the couch. Eyes shut, she lay listening to the sparrow-laced silence, smiling at the muted conversation from the passing joggers. Her cheek was cool with the new day, and she stretched, her gaze going to the kitchen. Something had woken her, but it hadn't been Haley. The kitchen held only silence. *And the playful canister set and matching dishcloths we picked out,* Meg thought as she sat up, her toes reaching to feel the bumps on the colorful throw they'd bought almost as an afterthought but which seemed to bring everything together.

Her sleepy smile lingered as she took in the pleasant living room opening up to the kitchen. She and Haley had finished unpacking last night, and the small apartment looked like a dream with the pale blue sheers at the window wall shifting in the breeze coming in from the balcony. The color went with the glass vase Meg had picked out, and the daisies she'd arranged within it looked like a piece of perfection.

Hands stretching to the ceiling, she stood, thinking that she'd never slept so well. No nightmares, no images of Austin broken and bloody, bleeding his life out in her car while she sat in the blessed stillness and did nothing.

Content, she folded the bedding up and stacked it on a nearby chair so she could put the new sunflower-graced pillows back on the couch where they belonged beside the Picasso-themed throw done in yarn. Turning, Meg's smile widened as she saw her canvas set up beside the window to catch the coming afternoon sun—right where she had envisioned it. Her brushes and pigments that she'd brought from home were arranged neatly on a small table beside it. There was even an adjustable artist's stool that Haley had insisted on buying after finding out she was moving in. Everything was arranged upon a soft, warm rug that Haley had picked out for just this reason.

Slowly Meg's smile faded. Her tools looked like clutter next to the clean precision of the rest of the apartment. No... not clutter, more like the toy box set up to keep the child happy and entertained.

Standing there in the cool breeze from the window, Meg felt a frown furrow her brow as she remembered Haley's oddly intense determination that everything on the rug be exactly how Meg wanted it. It was *her* spot, Haley had insisted, but now, seeing everything arranged just so, the rug looked like a dog blanket.

"Stop it, Meg. She just wanted to make sure you didn't lose the security deposit," she whispered, refusing to let herself ruin this.

Turning away, Meg shuffled into the bathroom, as quietly as she could. Her shorter hair was almost a shock as she stared at herself in the wide mirror. She never took her gaze off it as she brushed her teeth using Haley's cinnamon toothpaste. Anticipation quickened her fingers as she got dressed in one of her new outfits. Her mood restored, she looked at herself and called her black work shorts and breezy top good. Her feet were bare in her new sandals to show off her pedicure, and with a final flip of her hair, she adjusted the smooth length of Rorry's necklace to hide the clasp.

He'll be back tonight, she thought, letting her anticipation rise up to show in her eyes. What would he think of her moving in? A flash of anxiety pulled through her, and Meg drew her purse closer, pushing aside the guilt along with her empty diary as she searched for her meds. A bare three pills rattled as she opened the vial and used the water from the tap to wash one down.

Exhaling, Meg looked at herself in the mirror again, calmer as the overhead light hit her necklace to send shafts of gold about the small room. "I've got this," she whispered as she stuffed the pill vial back under her diary, glad she was going to see Dr. Jillium this afternoon to get more. Getting there and back without Haley knowing might be difficult, but if Meg stopped in right after class, Haley would never know.

With a final primp in the mirror, Meg went out, her thoughts on making coffee vanishing when the soft sounds of Haley and Rorry talking in the kitchen met her. Their give-and-take banter sounded like home, and Meg's pulse leapt.

"Rorry!" Beaming, Meg crossed the living room, glad now that she'd already folded up her sheets and stacked her pillows. Not to mention brushed her teeth and put on a wisp of makeup. "I didn't think you'd be back this soon. Did you miss your train?"

Haley uncrossed her arms from over her middle as Rorry saw Meg, his eyebrows rising. "Wow, you look great," he said, and Haley's somewhat cross expression eased into what might be pride.

"Didn't I tell you?" she said, smiling to make Meg feel as if she'd interrupted a conversation about her. "Good morning, Meg. You want some coffee?"

"Yes, please," Meg said, eager to use one of the cheerful mugs that Haley had bought yesterday. It had flowers enameled on the inside as well as out, and Meg had never seen anything so frivolous and charming. "What are you doing here?" she asked Rorry, then caught her breath, surprised when he gave her an expansive hug.

"I've been there and back. For once, the commute went smoothly. Wow. I can't get over how you look. That necklace is perfect on you."

"I love it. Thank you so much," she said again, heart pounding as she dropped back a step. There was a white pastry bag on the counter, and, giving her a wink, Rorry slid backwards and up to sit on the counter. Head down, he pulled the bag closer and opened it up.

"It's the wearer, not the jewelry," Haley said primly as she pulled the paper bag back and took out a muffin. "And what do you think about the apartment? We've been working on it all weekend. I think it's done. Meg, what do you think? Are we good?"

Meg watched Haley hand the bag back to Rorry, and he eagerly delved inside. Not a whisper of her anger remained. Perhaps Meg had imagined it. "Maybe," she said, never having thought that she'd ever be sorry about not getting to the mall. "It looks about done. A few more things here and there, but nothing we can't pick up when we see it."

His attention in the bag, Rorry took out two muffins. "I think it looks fabulous, but you, Meg, are amazing. It makes me wish I hadn't promised a girl that I'd be back before winter," he said as he extended a muffin to her.

"Oh. Thanks," she murmured, taking it.

"Haley says you're going to stay with us," Rorry said, and Meg hesitated over the muffin. It was lemon. Of course.

"Just until I find my own place," she said as she picked a crumble off the top and ate it.

"What about your old place?" Rorry asked, then took a huge bite of his muffin. "I thought you kicked your old boyfriend out. Is he getting ugly?" he said around his chewing.

Eyes rolling, Haley handed Rorry a napkin. "Why should she stay there when she can find something closer to us? Something he doesn't have a key to? A fresh start, right, Meg?"

"I suppose," Rorry said, and Meg nodded. Giving up on ever having another apple turnover again, she began to eat the lemon muffin. It was store bought, but good, and Meg watched in dread as Haley put spoonful after spoonful of sugar into one of those perfectly flowered mugs.

"Here you go," Haley said as she offered it to Meg, looking almost anxious. "What do you think? It's a new coffee maker. I've never used it before. Is it good?"

Meg eyed the sugar bomb before taking it, her desire to please Haley fighting with the urge to tell her she liked her coffee black, and only black. The need to keep Haley smiling won, and Meg took a sip, forcing a smile. "Perfect."

"Damn, I just can't get over how you look, Meg," Rorry said, and Meg pretended to take another sip. "You're like another person. No, same person, but the best parts shined up."

"Thanks." Meg set the coffee down, wondering if she should begin to cultivate a history of being klutzy and spill it in the sink.

Ankles crossed, Haley leaned back against the counter and sipped from her own flowered mug. "Meg, I'm sorry to do this to you, but I've got to go home for a few days. Family emergency."

Meg's eyes shot to Rorry. "Home?" she asked, setting her coffee down. "Is everything okay? Rorry just got back."

Leaning across the space, Haley gave Meg's hand a squeeze. "It should be, yes," she said as she dropped back, her eyes showing only a faint concern. "But I need to take care of a few things. Rorry will stay with you to keep Austin and that ugly homeless man away."

Meg was silent. Moving in with Haley and Rorry didn't sound as smart a decision if Haley wasn't going to be around to buffer Rorry. Sure, Rorry seemed to be a nice guy. He looked harmless as he sat on the counter, his long legs dangling down as he tried to unsuccessfully corral his crumbs and eat a second muffin at the same time. But she'd known him for only a few days.

"Meg, please say you'll stay and wait for me," Haley said, clearly recognizing her reticence. "I hate coming back to an empty apartment, and knowing you'll be here when I return makes me feel better about leaving. Besides, I don't want to leave unless I know you have someone to help if Austin or that horrid homeless man starts to bother you again."

There was that. A buffer between her and Austin would be more than nice. Going back to her old apartment wasn't an option. It was more than her pride could take. "Maybe I could go with you," Meg said, and Rorry started, beaming as he exchanged a wordless, encouraging look with Haley. "I could give my students a week-long assignment and blow them off. No one will say anything."

Her smile fond, Haley click-clacked across the kitchen to give Meg a hug, pulling her close for a brief second before letting her go to hold her at arm's length and just smile. "That's why I'm going, dear heart," she said, shocking Meg to stillness. "I want to ask if you can come and visit. If you want to, that is. Maybe for summer break. I could use a nice vacation, and I know you'd like it there. That's what Rorry was doing," she added as she glanced at him, her hands still on Meg's shoulders. "But my father is such a stickler about protocol. If we did things his way, you'd have to get a passport and fill out forms. I know if I could talk to him face to face and tell him how wonderful you are that he'd say yes. You *just have* to come visit," she implored, finally letting go to drop back a step. "You'd fit in so well, and my mother will adore your art. Everyone will."

Meg's pulse hammered. She didn't know what to say. It was what she wanted. Hell, she had suggested it herself just now. But Christopher's warning suddenly rose up. *Them.* Had he been talking about Haley and Rorry? But they weren't imaginary. They were real, as real as she was. Christopher was a loon hooked on a drug that had warped his vision of reality.

The same one I'm on, Meg thought, the three pills she had left heavy on her mind.

"Meg, it's going to be fine. I promise," Haley said as she threw the last of her muffin away in the decorator trash can with the electronic lid and wiped her hands on the pretty floral print flour-sack dishtowel. "I'll be gone just a few days. I already gave my own students a week-long assignment. Rorry will keep you company."

Haley smiled encouragingly. Beside her, still sitting on the counter, Rorry saluted Meg with his third muffin.

Meg hesitated. It felt like a failure to return to that brown apartment and Austin. She'd already told Dr. Jillium she had called it quits between them. "Why not?" Meg finally agreed, and Rorry grunted his approval.

"Thank you," Haley said, holding Meg's hand for an instant before turning away and taking her purse up from on the counter. "I'll see you in a few days, then. With good news. I promise!"

"You're leaving right now?" Meg blurted, then flushed at how needy it had sounded.

Haley, though, didn't seem to notice. "If I hurry, I can catch the transport that Rorry came in on," she said as she pulled him off the counter and gave him a quick hug. "Take care of Meg for me," she admonished him. "Can you handle it for a day or two?"

A day or two? Meg thought, disappointed.

"Ab-so-friggin-lutely," Rorry said as he reached for the bag of muffins again. "Meg, you want a ride into work? I love driving."

Meg was scrambling to catch up. Things were happening fast, but yes, she did need to go into class today. "You're not going to take Haley to the station?"

Haley shook her head as she checked inside her purse. "No," she said as she snapped it shut. "I'm going to walk it. By the time I get there, things might be ready to go. But thanks, anyway." She gave Meg a hug, and the scent of daisies and Queen Anne's lace seemed to rise up between them. "This is going to be so wonderful," she said as she dropped back, moving toward the door even as she spoke. "I promise, Meg. Bye, Rorry!"

"Later, Haley," he said, his head down as he finished his breakfast.

Meg watched her go, feeling somewhat abandoned as Haley breezed through the living room and then out the front door. It shut with a firm thump, and an unexpected stirring of excitement gripped Meg in the new silence. Alone with Rorry? Anything could happen.

Perfunctory Af**fection**

"I love what you two did with the apartment," Rorry said, and she looked up, noticing how tall he was.

"I didn't know you had a car," she said, and he smiled, putting a finger conspiratorially to the side of his nose.

"I thought I could drive yours," he said, and Meg blinked. The one that she and Austin shared. It was in her name, and parked right across the campus at her old place. The last thing she wanted was for Rorry to think she was afraid, and it was her car, damn it, gotten from her mom when she died. If she wasn't with Austin anymore, he had no right to drive it. She could tell Rorry that Austin had crumpled the front right panel, the one that she had left a mangled mess to remind herself not to run into any more trees.

"Why not?" she said, feeling breezy and daring as she set her coffee into the sink and threw her napkin away. "Give me a sec to get my purse."

Fifteen

The window was down, and the wind was a pleasant caress in Meg's hair as Rorry drove her back across campus. Her maroon Volvo had been right where it was supposed to be, and the thrill of stealing her own car was still running high in her. That Austin hadn't run out to stop them had been a relief. That Rorry hadn't said anything as he scrutinized the replaced, blue passenger side door on the otherwise maroon car, or the mangled, never-fixed passenger-side front panel had been even better. Feeling daring, she had the radio on louder than usual and the happy pop music made her smile.

To be honest, it would have been faster to have walked to class than hike across campus to get her car only to have to drive the entire way back. *But this?* she thought, beaming in the dappled sun as she brushed a spider out the open window and the wind ripped it away. This had been worth the trek across the quad. She had her car back. She and Haley could hit the stores hard now.

Rorry was a competent driver, one hand on the wheel, the other resting on the open window where the breeze shifted the hair on his arm. Noticing her attention on him, he smiled. "Go, go, go!" he said dramatically, echoing her words when she'd unlocked the car and they had piled in.

"Yeah, well, it was fun, wasn't it?" she said, and he laughed.

Feeling as if nothing could ruin her day, she sighed happily and gazed out the front window at the passing buildings and shops, playing with her gold pendant. It felt good to be out with Rorry. Being with Haley was empowering because Haley liked her ideas and they had fun together. But Rorry made her feel special, desirable, that she was worth something to more than just one person.

"I don't have anything to do this afternoon," he said, his measured, melodious voice going perfectly with the dappled shadows racing over the car. "Do you want to meet for lunch? Maybe Swanks?"

She felt as if she'd die and go to heaven if she walked into Swanks for lunch with Rorry, but her grip on her purse tightened. Stealing her own car had made her feel daring, but not that daring. "I'm going to be covered in paint by the end of class," she said, looking for an excuse. "There's only so much that a cleaner can do. But I like the idea of lunch.

How about we go somewhere else? Somewhere that will overlook a few smears of paint."

"They'll think you're quirky," Rorry countered. "No one will say anything. Haley told me they have a great French onion soup."

"They never *say* anything," Meg insisted. "That's half the problem," she added, unable to do it. Eating at Swanks with Haley at the end of a perfect day of shopping was different than walking in at noon after class, still in her work clothes and covered in paint. "Rorry, I'm not dressed for it. I'm sorry."

He turned to her, almost seeming shocked as he looked at what she was wearing, Slowly his brow furrowed. "I suppose you're right," he said, making her wonder if he'd forgotten that what she looked like mattered, too. "Then how about the putt-putt course?" he asked, but she thought his smile might be forced. "They make a mean hot dog."

"Sure. That's more in line with Monday." Lip between her teeth, she stared out at the passing buildings as she wondered what tax bracket he'd grown up in and felt inadequate. But even that couldn't dampen her mood and she sighed when her building loomed large. "You can park behind the building," she said, pointing at the small drive. "Right through there."

"Got it." Rorry smoothly turned the wheel, and Meg shivered as the shade of the building took them. It was damp back here where the nightly watering never saw the sun, and a tree frog trilled from one of the trees lining the lot. She looked up at the tops of the old oaks seeing the glint of webs. They were thick this year, but thankfully they seemed to prefer the sunnier reaches.

"I like paint under your nails," Rorry said out of the blue, and Meg flushed, her gaze dropping to her hands and the perfect red ovals that would likely be destroyed by the end of class. Austin had said nearly the same thing ages ago. "I forget that most people don't see it and think quirky, creative genius."

"I'm not a creative genius," she said, flushing, and Rorry smiled as he cruised for a spot.

"Genius is as genius does," Rorry said cryptically. "I can't wait to see you paint our dock at sunset with all the boats at rest. Like birds on the shore," he finished wistfully.

Still warm from the flattery, Meg scanned the lot. "It sounds lovely."

"The colors so sharp against each other," he said, his eyes on the ordered cars as he crept along. "It's like nothing I've seen here. I'd try painting it myself, but it comes out all wrong. Maybe I should try painting like you do. With only some of the colors."

Meg gave him a wan smile. "Maybe." Painting with only some of the colors wasn't really what she did. It was more like being able to see the whole from a part and knowing exactly what to leave in and what to leave out, tickling the brain to fill in the rest. It was likely that no two people ever saw her work the same way, which was an intriguing thought in itself.

"Do you think you could paint me something sometime?" Rorry said, as he turned to her. "If you want to?" he added, his expression anxious. "I don't care what it is."

"Sure." Meg's grip on the top of the window tightened. It was as if he was asking her to make him his favorite dessert and he didn't have the first idea of how a kitchen worked.

"Today, maybe?" he added when he saw her blasé attitude. "Or tonight. Tomorrow even."

At that, she laughed, touching his knee to reassure him she wasn't laughing at him. He looked so desperate for it, and that was as flattering as all hell. "I've been wanting to do the fountain," she said, thinking it would be prudent to have an example for the prompt she wanted to give her students. It would be frogs and lily pads today.

Rorry's expression lightened. "Oh, that would be great. Something that shows where we've been would be outstanding. Haley never lets us bring much when we leave, but I know she'd let me keep that. She likes your work as much as I do."

Meg's smile became stilted. She'd forgotten that they were leaving at the end of the semester. "There's a spot," she said, pointing, and Rorry immediately pulled in with the ease of long practice. One of the car's belts screamed in protest. It hadn't been fixed, either, and Meg winced, the sound never having bothered her before. Maybe she should do something about that.

"You don't have to paint if you don't want to, though," Rorry rushed, his eyes suddenly pinched. "We could go out on the lake, or the mall. Whatever."

"No, I could do with a little time on the canvas this afternoon." She smiled as Rorry turned the car off, but inside she was wondering how she was going to get to Dr. Jillium's for her next twenty-four hours of Fitrecepon without Rorry knowing about it. Lip curled under, she gathered her purse. "Thanks for the ride."

"No problem." He handed the key to her with an overdone flourish. "I should probably get my license renewed."

Meg looked up from dropping the key into her purse, her eyes wide. "You don't have a license?" she asked. He clearly knew how to drive.

"Not for here." Rorry opened the door, his long legs swinging to find the pavement. "It's hard when you have to keep updating your address."

"I suppose." Meg got out as well, her closing door sounding loud as it echoed against the buildings. The reminder that they wouldn't be here after winter sobered her. "It must be hard moving around so much."

Rorry shrugged, squinting at her across the top of the car. "I won't be doing it forever. And if all goes well, both

Haley and I might be able to stop moving soon." His smile widened. "See you in about four hours? Haley left me a market list. Do you want anything special?"

Meg's lips quirked, not surprised. The refrigerator was utterly empty. When and where Haley had gotten the sugar and coffee was a mystery. "No," she said, anxious to get in and start class. Stealing her car had almost made her late. "Why don't you take the car? The nearest grocery store is like half a mile away. Not a bad walk, but if you're carrying bags, it can take forever. Especially if you need everything." *Like sugar, and butter, and coffee.*

Head dropping, Rorry sighed. "Okay, you caught me. I'm not going shopping. I was going to talk to Austin, and I can't tool up to his place in your car. The man does have his pride, I suppose."

"You want to talk to Austin?" she blurted, the fear of the two of them meeting bringing her up short. She did *not* want Rorry to find out anything about her, how Austin had been living with her for three years making himself into her crutch, her weekly sessions with Dr. Jillium, and definitely not her new medication. "No. Rorry, please don't. I've got this handled."

"Someone needs to tell him to leave you alone," he grumbled, looking protective.

"And I did that," she said, pulse fast as she came around the car to meet him at the front. *Oh, God, if they ever meet, it will all come tumbling down,* she thought as she stood between Rorry and the mangled front. "It's not your problem. It's mine."

Squinting in the dappled sun, he took her hands. "One you shouldn't have to deal with."

Head down, she gathered her thoughts. "I understand what you're trying to do, but really, this is something I need to do on my own." She looked up, trying to impress him to back off and stay backed off. "It will be okay. He'd never hurt me." *No, he just enabled me to stay stuck where I was for three years.* "Promise me you'll leave him alone. Promise, or I'm not going into my class."

Rorry looked at her hands in his, and she breathed a sigh of relief when he finally muttered, "Okay. I promise. But I don't know what I'm going to do for the next few hours."

Smiling fondly, she rocked back, her hands slipping from his. "You could get your license renewed."

Rorry shrugged sheepishly. "I could get my license renewed," he echoed.

Meg's shoulders slumped in relief. "I'll see you for lunch," she said, and thinking that sticking with him for the entire day was probably a good idea. Maybe she could cut class short and be out to Dr. Jillium's and back before he returned to drive her home. It wasn't as if they could leave the car here overnight.

"Putt-putt," he said, pantomiming hitting a ball and making a little *tunk* of sound, and she gave him a little wave before turning to weave through the cars to the back door. Her confident pace faltered as she walked right into a spi-der-web. Warming, she turned to see if Rorry noticed, but he was already halfway to the street, his hands in his pock-ets and his head down.

Her building pass opened the back door, and she ghosted inside, the air conditioning dry and empty of the rich scents from outside. Unseen voices echoed in the wide corridors, and she hustled up the three flights of wide marble stairs to her sun-drenched studio class. She wasn't late yet, but it was close, and she smiled and met the eyes of everyone on the way, feeling good about where she was and what she was doing. Rorry wanted a special picture of the fountain, and she was already sketching it out in her mind.

No one noticed when she slipped into her room, her students busy comparing the work they'd done over the weekend or complaining that they hadn't had enough time. It was a little slice of heaven, and she went to the back of the room to put a few things she'd need for Rorry's picture into her purse before things got busy and she for-got. She was tucking the tin of cleaner away as she froze in a stunning realization.

She wasn't anxious about the class at all.

Exhaling, she turned to them, grateful for the meds that were finally letting her remember who she'd been before her mother had died.

"Okay, settle down," she said loudly, and they all looked up, someone actually swearing as they realized it was her. It only added to her confidence. "I see that not everyone has their three canvases that I assigned last Friday," she said as she strolled from the back sinks to the elevated instructor stage. Her shadow was long across the easels as she walked before the tall windows, and she couldn't help but smirk at the range of expressions from dismay to anxious.

"Uh, I didn't know we were supposed to bring them in," one student said.

"That's why it's called homework, Stan," she said, relieved she actually remembered his name. She was smiling to ease the bite of her words, and it felt good to be able to joke around with them. From the back, someone tittered, and a warm feeling suffused her.

But her pleasure that her humor was understood vanished when a familiar pace drew her attention out the window and she saw Austin stomping across the quad, his destination obvious. Her smile vanished, and she forced her hand down from her necklace. Clearly he was upset about the car, but it was hers, damn it, and they had broken up. Did he think that he got the car just because she didn't drive it?

Maybe I should have left him a note or texted him, she thought, suddenly feeling trapped. She just drove off with it leaving him to assume...what? What kind of a jerk does that to someone else? But she had been mad and somewhat of a coward, and watching his arms swing, she realized that hadn't changed.

The need to flee filled her. She didn't want to ruin this perfect class with an ugly argument in the hall where her students could hear. Perhaps she should take the opportunity to run out to Dr. Jillium's for her meds right now. She could be back in twenty minutes, avoiding Austin and getting her meds both.

Arms around her middle, she watched Austin, not caring if running made her a coward. "Okay," she said loudly to bring the class back to attention. "We're going to take our mid break right now so those of you who didn't bring in last Friday's assignment can retrieve them. I'm going to skip out for a moment," she said as she crossed the room quickly, purse in hand. "But I'll be back in twenty. I expect everyone to have their canvas or don't bother to come back."

"Oh, man..." one of the students griped, falling back against one of the long tables. "I've got more to do than paint all weekend."

"Then you do not belong in my class," Meg said as she bolted out the door and let it swing shut behind her. Her last sight was of two of her students frantically throwing pigment on canvas in a clear attempt to have something to share—as slipshod and purposeless as it would be—just so they wouldn't get kicked out. It was gratifying, both that she could make such a demand and that there were those who would try to cover their lapse just to stay involved. But Meg hardly had the state of mind to appreciate it as she raced down the now-empty marble steps and out into the damp parking lot.

Breath held, Meg looked toward the lot's entrance, then back to her car. In a burst of daring, she ran to the Volvo, head down as she dug in her purse for her keys. Austin had a key as well, and she didn't want to have to explain to Rorry why the car was gone if he took it. Rorry would probably want to confront Austin to get it back, and from there, everything would tumble down like cards.

Her fingers trembled as she yanked open the door and got in, fumbling to get the key in the ignition. She hadn't driven for three years. *I'm much better now,* she thought as the car started up with a loud rumble. The sudden blaring of the radio startled her, and Meg snapped it off, frantically checking behind her before lurching the car back out of the slot, a belt whining in protest.

"Meg!" Austin called, and Meg swore as she spotted him. Fumbling, she jammed the car into drive and lurched forward, tires squeaking on the wet pavement.

"Meg, wait!" Austin called as he ran to cut her off at the entrance. "I need to talk to you. I'm not mad about the car! I just want to talk."

Gasping, she jumped on the brakes when he darted across the entrance. The car lurched as her head swung, and her pulse hammered at the narrow miss. Shocked, she almost stalled the car, doing nothing as he grabbed the bottom of her open window, his eyes pinched in desperation. "I just want to talk," he said again, and her breath came fast. "Where are you going?"

"Somewhere you aren't." She squinted up at him in the dappled shade. She wanted this done and over. She couldn't live like this anymore. "Let go of the car, Austin. Let go, or I swear *I'll run you over!*"

The last was a veritable screech, and he let go, his eyes wide in shock as he dropped back.

She drove off in a squealing of tires and something thumping deep in her car's engine. Meg looked back as she bounced out onto the main street. The light ahead was just turning yellow, and she sped through it, heart pounding. She felt alive as she left him behind, eager to talk to Dr. Jillium and get a new set of meds. The persnickety woman might not even care that Meg had been ignoring her diary if she pulled up in her car.

Sixteen

xcitement hummed through Meg, the vibration of the rumbling engine pushing it up through her feet and all the way to her fingertips as she drove to Dr. Jillium's. It was more than odd to be behind the wheel after three years; it was exhilarating. The wind gusting through the window tugged her hair, and a long-absent sensation of independence had her hyper alert. She didn't even mind that her car was mechanically-off, noisy, something she'd never noticed when Austin drove it. Her attention was evenly divided between the campus's cramped, twisty roads before and behind her for any sign of Austin.

Her mood suddenly tarnished as a three-year-old memory spun up from nowhere, of her driving off the road and intentionally into a tree. She didn't even remember why she'd done it, other than she'd been despairing about something, overwhelmed, unable to cope, so desperate to feel something other than loss that pain had been a relief. The quiet afterward certainly had been.

Afterward, everything changed, and yet, nothing was different. Austin had been terrified, which, in light of her new understanding, might be why she'd never let him get the car fixed. She knew the reminder of that night bothered him, and it had probably been a passive aggressive way to punish him for keeping her this needy thing that required his presence to function.

Quite sure she wasn't ready to bring this new-found realization up with Dr. Jillium, Meg carefully pulled up to the curb and put the car into park only four spots down from her office. Meg wasn't that same person anymore. She knew the signs and could sidestep self-injury, but her old self lingered in the shadows, ready to pounce if she should falter. Always and ever she had to be vigilant to her past, lest she have no future.

Meg got out. Her grip tightened spasmodically on her purse as she looked down the street, the hard shape of the brush cleaner obvious through the fabric. She couldn't keep dodging Austin forever. But she didn't want to face him today. Not now.

Taking a deep breath, she jogged up the wide stone steps and hit the buzzer. "Dr. Jillium? It's me."

"Come on up, Meg. The door is open," came back immediately, and Meg pulled on the heavy glass door as a harsh tone hummed.

Perfunctory **Af**fection

She went in, the building's cool air somehow unpleasant after the moist warmth of the morning blowing through her hair. Her pace was fast as she took the smooth steps up to the third floor, giving the front door a perfunctory knock before going in. The living room was empty, and she unslung her purse from her shoulder as she crossed to the wide window to look down at her car. *No Austin.*

"Hi Dr. J," she said loudly at the small noise from the inner office. "I probably should have called, but I was in the area and I took a chance you'd be available." Her brow furrowed as she looked up the empty street. *Still no Austin.*

"Hi, Meg," Dr. Jillium's voice came back unseen. "Come on in. I'm just finishing some paperwork."

Mentally telling Austin to back off, Meg turned, shook out her hands, and went into the inner office. The stately woman was at her smaller desk, the windows that never opened already shuttered as if ready for a session. Dr. Jillium smiled as she looked up from putting her hand-written notes into a folder and closing it. Meg's own smile went stiff as she saw her name on it.

"You wouldn't believe the paperwork that goes with an experimental drug," Dr. Jillium said as she set a hand protectively on the file. "Wow. I don't think I've ever seen you look that sharp before. That haircut suits you. Special day?"

"No, but thank you." She wanted to get her pills and leave, but she gingerly sat on the front of a chair before the long coffee table. It wasn't her usual spot, and she hoped Dr. Jillium would take the hint that she was in a hurry. "I had it cut Saturday," she said as she felt the tips and wondered how it could have only been two days ago. It felt like an entire summer. "Right during the busy hours," she added when Dr. Jillium clearly waited for more.

"I'm very glad to hear that. How's work going?"

Meg set her purse on the low table, the clink of the brush cleaner obvious. "Good," she said. "Better than good. Everything is perfect. I drove today."

Dr. Jillium stood, her eyes going down to the street. "Congratulations," she said, looking at her car. "I know that's a big step."

Meg's brow furrowed. "Yes. Thank you. It feels good to be on the road again. I should probably get it fixed if I'm going to drive it."

Dr. Jillium's eyebrows rose at Meg's sour tone. "Do you want to talk about it?"

Meg shrugged, forcing herself not to look at the cabinet behind Dr. J's desk. "Not really. It wasn't a big deal once I got behind the wheel."

"I'm curious." Dr. Jillium sat on the edge of the front of her desk, arms crossed. "What prompted you?"

At least three lies, none of them convincing, rose up through Meg's thoughts, but she was mad at Austin, and if Dr. Jillium sided with her, she could dump the lingering guilt and get on with the breakup. "It's Austin," she finally said. "He's being a pain about me not wanting to live with him anymore. I wanted my car back, and I took it without telling him."

Dr. Jillium stood, her expressive eyebrows high. "Oh," she said as she moved back behind her desk and touched her tablet awake.

Meg sighed, glancing at the clock over the defunct fireplace, wishing she'd kept her mouth shut. A vague feeling of being threatened stole over her, but it was Austin who had the problem, not her. "It's as if he's stalking me," she said, and Dr. Jillium swiped through her tablet until settling on something. "I've told him to go away. Several times."

"That's positive." Dr. Jillium came back around her desk and sat down across from Meg. "That you are delineating a clear separation will further your progress immeasurably."

Resigned to being here for at least twenty minutes, Meg sat back and stilled her jiggling foot before Dr. Jillium wrote that down. "It felt good at the time," she admitted. "But when the excitement wore off, I was left wondering if I'm making a mistake. What's the harm in listening to him? I mean, it's been three years. Don't I owe him a few minutes if only to give him a reason why?"

"Perhaps you could write down how you feel in a letter," Dr. Jillium said, and it was all Meg could do to not roll her eyes. "That way, you have closure, and he won't bother you anymore."

"A letter?" Meg echoed, her voice flat. "Do you really think that will do it?"

Dr. J shrugged. "It will if you want it to. Would you like to compose it together?"

A letter *would* be court-worthy, documented evidence that she'd asked him to leave her alone. Maybe that was what Dr. Jillium was after. "No," Meg said, feeling the pinch of time. "I should do it myself," she added when Dr. Jillium crossed her legs disapprovingly. "Mail it off. Be done with it. Besides, I really have to get back to class. I gave them twenty minutes to get their homework up and displayed. I didn't realize you'd want to talk."

Dr. Jillium glanced at the wall clock, her head bobbing. "That's right. Monday, Wednesday, and Friday. Let me get your meds then, and we can talk more tomorrow."

She rose, and Meg stifled her impatience as Dr. Jillium went to the cabinet and unlocked it with a key on her car's fob. Taking out a small vial, she locked it back up again before turning to flip Meg's paper file open. "Thank you again for being so amendable to coming in like this," she said, head down as she copied a number on the vial into Meg's file. "I know it's inconvenient."

Realizing her hands were clasped, Meg forced them flat on her knees. "No worries. You're only a ten-minute walk away."

Her expression pleasant, Dr. Jillium crossed the office, vial in hand. "Here you go. Again, I'm sorry we have to do this day by day, but until Chris is found, I'd feel more comfortable. He can't be allowed any more Fitrecepon, and a week's worth might damage him beyond recovery."

"It's not a problem." Meg took it, dropping it in her purse as she stood. "He seems as if he needs a lot of help," she said, fiddling with her new necklace.

"I blame myself," Dr. Jillium said, and Meg's escape to the door slowed from curiosity. "He seemed as if he was handling it and that the Fitrecepon was doing him a lot of good. He'd become more outgoing, positive about the future. Had even made a few friends that he'd been spending time with. Almost a new person." Hesitating, Dr. Jillium looked Meg up and down. "It all began to fall apart right about the time he took off his wedding ring. He said it was making his finger itch, but the more I think about it, the more I think it was just an excuse. I don't think he was having an allergic reaction at all. Perhaps he was just afraid to admit that he'd let his wife and child go and blaming it on a rash was easier."

Meg clasped her purse before her like a fig leaf. "People are funny like that."

"Aren't they?" Dr. Jillium stood before the long couch, an odd look on her face. "Meg, I don't want to change your dosage, but we might want to consider easing back on how often you take them. Can I see your log? It will only take a few minutes."

"Ah, I didn't bring it," she lied. "Is tomorrow okay?" She could jot down a few things tonight. Write down when she'd been taking them, and why.

"It's in your purse," Dr. Jillium said helpfully. "I saw it when you put the Fitrecepon in it." Meg froze, and seeing it, Dr. Jillium sighed in disappointment. "You haven't been keeping up with your log, have you," she accused, and Meg winced.

"I know I've only been taking four a day," Meg said, voice high. "One in the morning, one at night, and two during the day. I've done all the other homework."

Dr. Jillium sat back on the tall arm of the couch. "Meg, we aren't even in clinical trials. I need this information to justify making it available to other people who need it. The intent was to have a record of the changes in your behavior so we could make a better guess as to Fitrecepon's therapeutic duration and its long-term effect."

"I can tell you exactly what the effect is. It works! Look at me!" Meg exclaimed, gesturing down at herself.

"I am," she said calmly. "And I'm concerned that you haven't been keeping a record of your emotions. The changes in the brain can become permanent, so it's important that they are the right ones."

"Dr. J..." Meg almost whined, and then she turned when the unseen door to the apartment opened and Austin called out, "Dr. Jillium? Is Meg here? I just want to talk to her for five minutes. Just five minutes, and I promise I'll never bother her again."

"Son of a bitch..." Meg whispered.

"Meg?" Dr. Jillium questioned when Meg retreated deeper into the office until her back was to the window, staring at the office door as if it was the gateway to hell.

"It's Austin," she said bitterly, and Dr. Jillium's lips parted in shock before she steeled her expression back to a neutral calm. "This is all Austin's fault. Everything would be perfect if he'd just leave me alone!"

"I agree," her psychiatrist said. "But we need to talk this out before I can give you any more Fitrecepon."

Meg spun, Austin almost forgotten in her sudden panic. She was going to withhold her meds because of Austin? He was *stalking* her. "But this is his fault!" she exclaimed, only to turn back to the door when Austin scuffed to a halt in the threshold, looking hot and ragged for having run it, probably.

"This is *not* my fault," he said hotly, then pointed at Dr. J, the woman's eyes wide as she stared at Meg. "Everything was fine until the Fitrecepon," Austin said as he limped in. "It was under control. Now it's new shoes, new dress, new friends, new attitude."

"You think it's too fast?" Dr. Jillium said, but she was still looking at Meg, and Meg held her elbows, nervous. "That's why I want to lower the meds. Just until everything catches up."

Kim Harrison

"Catches up?" Austin exclaimed. "Are you serious?"

Dr. Jillium's lips pressed. "Okay. I'm going to get you something to drink, and we can sit down and talk this out." Pushing into motion, she headed for the kitchen. Meg followed, not liking the ugly look Austin had. It was mean. She'd never seen it before, and it scared her.

"So you can put something into it and make all of this go away?" he said bitterly, not moving out of the threshold. "Not this time," he said, and Meg reached out, grabbing Dr. Jillium's elbow, yanking her back before Austin did something awful.

"Hey!" the woman protested as she swung around and back into the room, stumbling to catch her balance.

"Stay out of my way," Austin threatened, and Meg followed him, panicked as he stomped over to the cabinet behind the desk. *He wouldn't destroy the Fitrecepon, would he?* she thought as he rattled the door to find it locked.

"Meg. Sit down. We need to talk," Dr. Jillium said, her voice firm but shaken. "I'm sorry about your class. I'll call your supervisor later today and explain."

Damn it, Austin, you're ruining everything, Meg thought as Austin rattled the cabinet's door again. Dr. Jillium was going to cut her off, and it was all Austin's fault. She should have just run him over when she had the chance.

"This is not going to happen." Austin said bitterly.

Meg's eyes widened as he made a fist, his eyes fixed on the cabinet's glass door. "Austin, no!" she cried, lurching forward as he slammed it into the glass. The antique glass shattered, and she fell back against Dr. Jillium's desk, shocked as he used the stapler to knock the remaining shards away, his hand a bloodied mess.

Standing beside the window, Dr. Jillium took out her phone, her expression grim.

"What are you doing!" Meg demanded as Austin yanked her forward, grabbed the paint thinner out of her purse, and shoved her back.

"I'm calling 911." Her lips pressed tight in anger, Dr. Jillium put her cell phone to her ear.

"Like hell you are," Austin said, and Meg stood, transfixed as he threw the heavy tin of paint thinner at her.

"Dr. Jillium!" Meg shrieked, and she looked up, eyes widening as the tin hit her square on the temple.

Dr. Jillium dropped like a stone, the phone spilling from her fingers to slide across the flat carpet.

"911. Please state your emergency," came from the speaker, and Meg ran to Dr. Jillium, crouching to give the woman a shake. She was breathing, but unconscious. Angry, Meg took the can of paint thinner and stood. It was red with Austin's blood, and it stained her hand.

"What are you doing!" she exclaimed, furious as she closed the gap between them. "Stop it. Just stop it! You're going to ruin everything!"

"I'm not the one ruining it." Austin's expression was ugly as he jerked the can of paint thinner out of her hand. "You are."

Kim Harrison

"Austin, stop!" she said, horrified as he unscrewed the cap and doused the cabinet, inside and out. "Austin!" she shrieked as, with a malevolent smile, he lit his lighter and tossed it in. With a whoosh, the cabinet was engulfed in flames. A thick, black smoke rolled out and up, covering the ceiling frighteningly fast. With a snap, the glass sides began to crack and pop. "My God! What are you doing!"

Austin tossed the lighter onto the desk. "I'm trying to save us," he said, eyes holding a heavy anger. "It's those damn pills, Meg. They're driving you away from me. Without you, I'm nothing. I can't let that happen."

Ticked, Meg stood toe to toe with him. "I like who I am when I'm on them," she asserted hotly. "What is your problem! You're the reason I'm such a mess! You kept me weak and helpless for three years. Well, I'm done with that. Done! Get out!"

He turned to look at the cabinet, the interior a flaming hell. "You'll be back," he said in a perverse satisfaction. Turning on a heel, he walked out.

Meg coughed, squinting through the smoke at the cabinet. The vials weren't on fire...yet. Heart pounding, she screwed up her courage and reached in, yelping as her hand felt the heat. Two vials rolled onto the floor. Meg pounced on them, shocked at how much cooler and cleaner the air was at the floor.

Eyes watering, she dropped to her knees, shoving the vials into her purse before crawling to Dr. Jillium. She could hear sirens outside. "Austin, you little bastard!" she shouted, and then, hanging her purse around her neck, she grabbed the woman by her shoulders and dragged her to the door.

Smoke filled the outer room. Alarms were going off all over the entire building, and she could hear people shouting in the hall, their voices high as they realized it was for real. "What the hell is the matter with you, Austin," she whispered, watering eyes clamped shut as she pulled Dr. Jillium through the waiting area. She fumbled at the door, and smoke billowed into the hall when she finally got it open. Choking, she rose, hunched as she dragged Dr. Jillium down the hall.

A looming shadow on the stairs suddenly appeared, and she shrieked, terrified it was Austin until she realized it was a fireman. "Help me!" she cried out, and the man flipped his face shield up.

A fresh-scrubbed face squinted at her before he pushed past and hoisted Dr. Jillium into a carry. "Is there anyone else in there?" he asked, and Meg turned to look, smoke and heat billowing out of Dr. Jillium's office.

"No," she said, remembering Austin's ugly expression when he left them. Then she gasped as he pushed her into motion down the stairs. "Did you see him? He ran out the door right before me."

"Who?" the fireman said, and Meg slowed, sucking in the cooler, cleaner air like water.

Kim Harrison

This was definitely going to make the news. She didn't want to have to explain to Haley and Rorry that it was her old boyfriend who torched Dr. Jillium's office, much less why she was there, but Dr. Jillium knew who Austin was, and as soon as she regained consciousness, the truth would be out. "My old boyfriend," she said, feeling as if she was betraying Austin, but he'd knocked Dr. Jillium out and tried to burn the building down along with her drug supply. "He's the one who started the fire. Is Dr. Jillium going to be okay?"

"We'll do what we can," he said, then pressed Meg against the stairway wall to make room for the two firemen dragging a hose upstairs. "Room of origin is clear!" he shouted after them, and a crackled response came back on his headset.

"Is she going to be okay?" Meg demanded again, and the fireman got her moving downstairs.

"I'm sure she'll be fine," he said, and then Meg was blinking, staring as she came out and into chaos. People were clustered across the road, most of them on their phones as they rubbernecked. An ambulance was just pulling up, joining the two fire trucks already on scene. Three cop cars were on hand, two blocking off either end of the street.

"Here! Over here! Smoke inhalation and blunt trauma to the head!" the fireman called, but the two paramedics were already on their way, a gurney rattling over the uneven sidewalk.

Perfunctory **Af**fection

Meg held her burned hand close, gaze fixed on Dr. Jillium. "She's got to be okay," Meg said, and the fireman smiled encouragingly.

"She seems stable," he said, then relinquished her to the paramedics, his voice serious as he told them what he knew.

That really wasn't what Meg wanted to hear. Guilt about the meds in her purse kept her eyes down, but if she hadn't taken the time to get them, who knew when or if she'd ever have access again? Maybe that had been the only stash?

Burned hand held close to her middle, she watched Dr. Jillium loaded into the back of the ambulance. It didn't drive away, and almost immediately, one man hopped back out and made a beeline back to her.

"Ma'am?" the paramedic called, a portable oxygen generator and mask in his grip.

Like thunder, reality crashed down to make her knees watery. Austin had almost killed them both. He had set fire to the building and walked out, leaving her to drag Dr. Jillium to safety. And why? Because she'd finally admitted he was a crutch and had left him so she could be something other than that weak, needy half-person he had wanted her to be.

"I'm okay," she protested as she clutched her purse, and the fireman eased her unresisting to sit on the grass outside the building. People were still coming out with their arms full of whatever they thought they'd miss the most, arguing when the police wouldn't let them go back in for more. She

Kim Harrison

didn't know any of the residents, and she scanned the street for a sign of Austin. The urge to get in her car and drive away was almost an ache, but even if she could get to her car, she wouldn't be able to get past the fire trucks.

"Let me slip this on," the paramedic said as he knelt beside her, and she felt she didn't deserve his kindness.

"Really, I'm okay," she said again, but he didn't listen, looping the mask into place. "We got out before the fire was too bad."

"Humor me then," he said with a smile, and she looked up, the mask feeling alien as it fitted over her face. The air was tasteless, somehow, and she breathed slowly.

"You'll be fine now," the fireman said, then lumbered over to the cops, his loud voice calling familiarly to them.

"It's a good thing you were there to get her out," the paramedic said as he tightened one of the elastic straps.

"I hope she thinks so when she wakes up," Meg said sourly, her words echoing oddly behind the oxygen mask. Her hand stung, and she tried to hide it and Austin's blood as the paramedic took her pulse and blood pressure.

"How are you feeling? Do you need to lie down?" the man asked, and she looked up, feeling sick to her stomach. "Shock is a funny thing," he added as he gently pried her burned arm from her middle so he could get a better look. "Go ahead. Lay down before you fall over. I'll get your hand cleaned up. No, keep the mask on," he said. "You look a little pale."

"I'm okay," she insisted, refusing to lie down, as she clutched her bag tight, averting her gaze as he poked and prodded.

"It doesn't look too bad," he said, and she relaxed at his kind smile. "I think a spray anesthetic will help more than anything. Hang on. This won't take long. What's your name?"

"Meg," she breathed, and the mask fogged up. "Meg Seton. Is Dr. Jillium going to be okay?"

He nodded as he sprayed something cool on her hand, and her shoulders eased in relief. "I think so. You got her out in time. How did she hit her head?"

The image of Austin's face screwed up in anger flashed through her. Fear that he might come after her if she brought him into it was a tight warning, and she dropped her gaze, watching the man wrap the last layer of gauze around her hand. Slowly she took the mask off, the straps tugging at her hair. Her smooth curls were going to smell like smoke, and she felt depressed.

"I'm being stalked by my old boyfriend," she said, though embarrassed she hadn't done anything wrong. "He was arguing with Dr. Jillium, and when she called 911, he threw my can of paint thinner at her. I teach painting at the university and I was on my way back to class. He dumped it in her office, lit it, then walked out."

"Ah, do you feel up to telling that to police before you leave?" the paramedic asked, and she nodded as her shoulders crept back up around her ears. "Good, because otherwise, I'm going to insist that you get checked in if only for your own safety, and I don't think this is so bad that we need to."

Her smile turned to relief, and she looked at her hand swaddled up in a neat bandage. Her wince when she tried to flex it vanished as the windows to Dr. Jillium's office suddenly burst out, glass tinkling down to briefly shut up the residents still crabbing about trying to go back in. Smoke and fire rolled out, then subsided.

"It's lucky you were there to pull Dr. Jillium to safety," the paramedic said, and Meg nodded, glad she had salvaged more than one day's worth of meds. Dr. Jillium's office was a total loss. All those records, gone. "Promise me you'll get your hand looked at by your regular doctor within twenty-four hours. Infection is a real possibility with a wound like that."

Meg flexed her hand again, thinking there was less pain this time. "Thank you, I will."

"Okay." He stood, motioning for her to keep the oxygen mask when she began gathering it up for him. "Keep it until you leave. Just in case you need it," he said, then beckoned the nearby cop. "Officer Lakes will take your statement. He's a nice guy."

"Thank you," she said softly, but the paramedic was already jogging away to check on everyone clustered in the tiny front lawn.

Perfunctory **Af**fection

Officer Lake made one final comment to the fireman who had gotten her down the stairs, and ambled over, his stance wide and his arms swinging to avoid the clutter strapped around his waist. "Are you okay, ma'am?" he asked, squinting down at her in the sun, and Meg stood.

"I should be, yes," she said, coughing as she brandished her gauze-wrapped hand.

"Is it true you know the man who started the fire?" Officer Lake said, and she winced, wishing she could just lie and have all of this go away, but she knew that Dr. Jillium wouldn't go along with it.

"I thought I did, but I guess not," she said, then added, "He's my ex-boyfriend. Austin Bonnard," when Officer Lake frowned. It was the third time she had said it, but it wasn't any easier. "He used my brush-cleaning solution to set fire to her office. I don't think he meant to hurt anyone." But inside, she knew he had.

"Ma'am, I'm going to need your cell number. Do you have someone to stay with tonight?" Officer Lake asked as he took out a tiny spiral notebook.

Meg's focus went distant down the road, hoping Austin was long gone but her luck had never been that good. "I do. Thank you," she said, quite sure she wasn't going to tell Rorry and Haley about this. Ever.

Seventeen

Meg's pulse was slow and her breathing even. Her hand twinged at the pinch of the gauze as she smeared the dark pigment across the background of a goldish, sunset pink. The warmth of the low sun beat upon her as she sat with her back to the balcony windows. It illuminated her canvas with a shocking light, bouncing up from her work and filling her with the peace she craved.

And still…the gnawing need of anxiety threatened to crawl up her feet, following the band of sun inexorably rising from her ankles, to her calves, and finally her hips as the sun set. The "knowing" that she had to be done before the sun vanished was a terrifying goad, one she couldn't explain but which was as real as the rug that Haley had bought for her under her feet.

She'd called Rorry shortly after giving her statement to the police. Avoiding any mention of the fire, she simply told him she would drive herself home after class and not to bother coming to get her. The scant intervening hour she spent at the coffee shop drinking overly sweet coffee had only spun her thoughts faster until she had spilled into the sanctuary that she and Haley had made with only one need: to forget. Her goal wasn't to numb, but to obliterate it in an outpouring of expression.

And so she painted.

Rorry was in the adjoining kitchen, the soft sounds of him making coffee hardly noticed. His presence was comforting by its very unobtrusiveness. Meg's lips pressed as she heard the clink of a spoon stirring in sugar, but she said nothing. Her hand ached, and the gauze wrapping made her grip chancy. The resultant awkwardness showed in her brush strokes, but it only added to the feel of the piece, making it more authentic as she mixed her old, pre-accident style with her new to get something amazingly unexpected.

"One cup of coffee for the lady," Rorry said softly, and she jumped, startled as he set the enameled flower mug beside her mason jar of brushes.

"Thank you." Smile fixed in place, she sighed before taking a sip. *At least it's hot*, she thought, wincing at how sweet it was. She missed her bitter brew, but it was a small price to pay for their friendship. She'd never go back to the way things were. Cinnamon toothpaste and sweet coffee—a gold necklace instead of a silver ring from a man who had made her life a prison so he would feel empowered. She'd take that any day, and twice on Sunday.

"How's your hand?" Rorry asked, hovering close with a serious frown. "If it hurts, you don't have to paint."

"It's fine." Meg set the coffee down and flexed her fingers, thinking it had been an odd thing to say, as if he was doing her a favor, by telling her she didn't have to paint. "They're going to get the water heater in my class looked at and turned down. Really, Rorry, it's fine," she said, the lie that she'd burned her hand while washing out brushes coming easy. Eyes on her canvas, she felt her ears burn. Anyone who knew anything would realize that you don't wash oil brushes with hot water, but a solvent. *A flammable solvent.*

She stiffened when Rorry went behind her to get a better look and his shadow fell cold over her. "Sorry," he said, shifting until the sun warmed her again. Her feet and legs were cool, and a whisper of groundless anxiety flickered through her as the band of shadow rose. "My God, Meg. That is incredibly beautiful."

"Thank you," she said, gazing at it in agreement even as she continued to add a wisp of paint to hint at a boat at the quay.

"But...the mountains are higher in Perfection," he said, and she couldn't decide if he was teasing her or not. "The sun catches them wa-a-a-ay up there," he said, pointing. "Even when the bay is in dark shadow."

"Like this?" she said coyly, adding a few strokes over the background of sunset to heighten the mountains.

"Perfect," Rorry said around a heartfelt sigh, and Meg let her brush come to rest. Together, they evaluated it. The reaches were gold, blue, pink, and red, and the lower bay in the shadow was purple, gold, and silver with winking lights. The boats at the quay were mere suggestions of broken lines in her new style, and looking at it, it seemed to her as if she had painted a million simultaneous sunsets overlapping themselves to make one firm image. The boats and quay were a subliminal suggestion, a mere flash in the span of time.

It was undoubtedly her best work, the blending of her previous, dull landscapes, and her new, disjointed style creating into a real/not real image that drew and held the eye and mind, expanding both into what had been, what might be, what is but has no meaning.

"Perfect," Rorry said again, and Meg started, having forgotten he was there, so lost was she.

"I'm glad you like it," she said, as she set her brush down and wondered how she was going to tactfully get rid of that coffee. Rorry seemed to relax at the click of the brush into the mason jar, his lanky form sliding out from behind her. "Any thoughts about dinner?" she asked, pretending to take a sip.

Rorry shrugged. "Order in?"

"Sounds good to me," she said, seeing as there was still nothing in the fridge, and they both looked up when the key sounded in the lock.

"Haley!" Meg exclaimed as the woman breezed in, and Meg stood, the feeling of guilt both sudden and shocking. Her new manicure was spoiled, and she felt a mess. "Did you miss your train?"

Rorry's eyes were wide in surprise. "You got an answer already?"

A thrill jolted through Meg. An answer? For her coming to visit? Haley had been there and back already?

But Meg's excitement faltered at Haley's continued, angry, irate expression. "Is everything okay?" Meg asked in a small voice, and Haley tossed her purse to a nearby chair.

"Of course it is." Mood odd, Haley crossed the room and gave Meg an absent-feeling hug. "Rorry, can I have a word with you?" The woman's eyes dropped to the canvas, not a hint of her emotion showing as she looked at it.

"She wanted to paint," Rorry said quickly. "I didn't make her do it."

"Now?" Haley said stiffly as she paced into the kitchen and turned to wait.

Rorry and Meg exchanged a quick, worried look, and Meg hid her ruined nails behind her back. "Sure." Rorry gave Meg's shoulder a light touch before he followed Haley into the brightly-lit kitchen, the whimsical chickens and wire baskets with their ceramic eggs looking fake somehow.

Meg slowly sat back down, her hand going cool where she scrubbed the solvent-soaked rag to get rid of the paint. The red of sunset had stained her, muddying the sterile bandage. It wouldn't come clean, and her nails, she realized, were ruined.

Creation is messy and ugly. They were Christopher's words, and she tossed the rag beside the mason jar, wondering if Haley was upset about the untidy state of her and her corner of the living room. Uneasy, she tried to scrape the paint out from under her nails. Haley had hardly given her canvas a glance. No...she had looked at it, but it wasn't in approval. *Did I do something wrong?*

Suddenly Meg felt as if she was a dog who had soiled the carpet right in front of the door. Her eyes went to the canvas. Maybe it wasn't her best work.

"I leave you alone with her for one day, and look what happened," Haley said softly, and Meg began trying to clean the long-stained handles of the brushes.

"Nothing happened. I swear," Rorry said, mystified. "She went to work. She drove back. We've been here all afternoon. She wanted her car, we got it. Nothing happened."

"This isn't about her car," Haley said tightly.

Is she worried about my hand? Meg wondered. Head rising, she took a breath to tell Haley she was okay, but then stopped, shocked at Haley's utter anger as she all but pinned Rorry to the cupboards. She felt a wash of relief, then guilt, that she wasn't the one she was mad at.

Rorry was red-faced and apologetic, even as he was confused. "We've been here all afternoon," he coaxed, and Haley's eyes narrowed, her quick breath to berate him held when he added, "She's painted a beautiful picture. You haven't even looked at it."

Haley seemed to hesitate as she realized Meg was standing alone by her picture. It made Meg feel like a little kid hearing Mom and Dad argue and knowing it's about her. But the brushes wouldn't get clean, and finally Meg dropped them into the jar.

Haley took Rorry's shoulder and turned him away. "What about while she was at class?" she said, and a cold feeling slipped over Meg. "Did she tell you what happened when she was supposed to be at class? It's done, Rorry. She ruined herself."

Meg froze. Haley knew about the fire? How? She'd said there was no incoming news into Perfection. "My hand will be fine," Meg said, afraid to move from the last of the sun, fearing it would be the last she'd ever see. "I'm getting it looked at tomorrow. Really, it's fine. I can paint."

But Haley didn't seem to hear her. "It's done," Haley said, and Rorry shook his head in bewilderment. "She could have killed Jillium, and now they want nothing to do with her. She's too unpredictable."

Meg's lips parted. Haley knew Dr. Jillium? Then Meg hesitated. Haley thought *she* had set the fire? Chest tight, Meg stepped forward to explain, her words faltering at Haley's anger.

"We've never had a chance like this," Haley said. "Ever. They're livid that Fitrecepon might be taken out of trials because of her. We'll have to go back to aristocratic, untalented debutantes and broken addicts wasted on opium."

Meg retreated until her back hit the window wall, cold in the setting sun. *Haley knew about Fitrecepon?*

"I don't understand," Rorry doggedly protested. "We've been here all afternoon."

Haley crossed her arms over her chest. "While you thought she was at class, she burned down Jillium's office."

Meg froze, the fear and guilt hitting her so hard she couldn't breathe.

"Is she dead?" Rorry asked, his confusion shifting to a frightened alarm.

"No." Arms over her chest, Haley seemed to relax. "She pulled Jillium out. God knows why."

Meg pushed away from the glass window, her knees wobbly as she gathered herself. "That wasn't me," she said, voice warbling, and both Rorry and Haley spun as if having forgotten she was there, or shocked maybe that she'd dared to interrupt. "I mean, I pulled her out," Meg said hesitantly. "But Austin was the one that went bad-boyfriend and torched her office."

Perfunctory Affection

Silence grew as they stared at her, and feeling ill, Meg sat down. Everything she had wanted to hide from Haley was out. She'd as much as admitted she was a basket case, broken and not deserving of friends as beautiful as them.

Her head was down, but she heard Haley tell Rorry to stay where he was and the soft click of her sandals on the tile. Haley's calm presence sidled up to Meg's side, and still she couldn't look up.

"I'm sorry, Meg," Haley said, sounding truly apologetic. "You can't come to Perfection. Now, or ever. You're too dangerous."

Dangerous? Meg looked up, anger pushing out the guilt that she'd tried to hide who she really was. "Why?" she blurted. "Because I have a crazy boyfriend? He's the one that torched the place, not me. Why is everyone blaming me for things that he is doing?"

Haley gazed at her canvas with an odd look of longing and anger. "Austin has been dead for three years, Meg. You're the one who burned her office."

Meg sat for a moment absorbing that, a dizzy sensation spiraling up and out from her gut. "What? Are you crazy?" Stomach cramping, she looked at Rorry expecting to see outrage or maybe confusion, but he hadn't moved, still standing sideways to them with his back against the empty fridge, his fingers pressed into his forehead as if he had a headache.

Haley crouched down to put her eyes level with Meg, but her gaze never left the canvas. It was a hungry look, desperate almost, and Meg shivered.

"When you ran into that tree three years ago to feel something?" Haley said softly, almost in disinterest, "He died. You didn't. Your guilt invented a way to ignore it. You've been living in that dull brown apartment full of his things for the last three years, pretending he was still with you so you wouldn't have to face that you were the reason he died."

Heart pounding, Meg stood, thinking this was cruel. "How do you know about my accident?" she accused. "I never told you. Did Dr. Jillium tell you? Is this some kind of perverted therapy? Are you working for her? Are both of you!"

Haley stood and backed up, her expression one of sadness as she shook her head. "No, but Jillium's new medication does more than bring your latent hallucinations to reality so you can deal with them. It lets other things in too."

"I'm sorry, Haley," Rorry said from the kitchen. "I should have watched her more closely. This is my fault."

Her perfect lips pressed, Haley turned away as if Meg no longer existed. "It's my fault. I shouldn't have left. I knew better. She was doing so well that I misjudged her. This will not reflect on you. I'll make sure they know that. They've already scheduling an inquiry. We have to go back tonight."

Meg hated his relieved but guilty look. "What the hell is wrong with you people?" she accused, her arms around her aching middle as she stood between the balcony and her canvas, between reality and the unreal. "Austin is not dead."

Looking tired, Haley sat on the couch and took off her sandals. "Think it through, Meg," she said, as first one, then the second hit the floor. "Let the Fitrecepon finish its work. He's dead. *You* knocked Jillium out. *You* set the fire. *You* broke the glass and took all her meds, afraid that she was going to cut you off. Your hand is gashed, not burned. Look at it. *Look at it!*" she demanded louder, when Meg shook her head, afraid to.

"It was Austin," she whispered, scared. "He was trying to destroy my medication so I wouldn't leave him."

Haley looked at her, her elbows on her knees. "Because it was forcing you to realize he was a delusion. You were already taking steps to leave him behind. Eventually you would be able to accept the truth and Jillium would have helped you through it." A sad, disappointed smile settled into Haley's face. "Or you could have come to Perfection and been adored, but that isn't going to happen now."

Shocked, Meg just stared. Then she jerked, her jaw clenching as she found a better answer. Who was she going to believe? Three years of therapy, or some blond bitch she hadn't known two days ago? "What is wrong with you people?" she said as she grabbed her jar of brushes and her canvas, finding strength in them. "If you don't want me to live here, just say so."

Breath fast, Meg stomped across the room, shoving her brushes into her purse and tucking it under her arm.

"Haley, she's leaving," Rorry said plaintively, but Haley just sat on the couch.

"Let her go," Haley said. "She almost killed someone to preserve her delusion. She's too dangerous for Perfection."

"But she's taking the picture," he protested, and Meg's anger flared.

"Is that what I am to you?" she said hotly. Fumbling at the door, she left, slamming it behind her. She had to talk to Dr. Jillium. Austin was real. Why Haley and Rorry said he wasn't was a cruel joke.

Unless they were working with Dr. Jillium? They hadn't shown up until the Fitrecepon, and they knew things they shouldn't.

Never, she asserted, and then a cold wash of fear almost made her stumble on the stairs. Meg leaned into the wall as another option rose up to explain Haley's words. Was she turning into Christopher? Had she overdosed on Fitrecepon? Was this a "bad reaction?"

"No," she whispered, scared as she looked at Haley's closed apartment door. "Everything tastes the same," she mumbled aloud. "I'm not sleepwalking. I'm better than I was before. How can this be wrong?"

But she was drinking coffee that was too sweet. She had changed her toothpaste, and she had taken off her silver ring and necklace.

Perfunctory **Af**fection

Your hand is gashed, not burned, echoed in her thoughts, and Meg froze, jerking to a stop and staring at the red-smeared gauze as she reached for the handle of the building's door. Was it red paint, or blood?

Scared, she clutched her necklace, jolted when her fingers found Rorry's fractured golden drop instead of her mother's jewel-decked palette. *What have I done?*

Gasping, she tried to yank the pendent off, almost panicking when it took two tugs to break the chain. With a cry of frustration, she threw it into a corner of the stairwell. Shoving the door open, she raced down to the sidewalk and into the dusky twilight. She had changed to please Haley, but she had changed.

Can you see them? Can you see them, yet? echoed in her mind, and she stifled a tiny shriek, hands waving as she ran through a spider filament stretching across the sidewalk. Moths were fluttering about the streetlights, and Meg ran to her car. There was a warning in the frog song coming from the nearby lake.

Dr. Jillium would know.

Eighteen

She'd known what was real before Dr. Jillium increased her meds. Of that Meg was certain. Beyond that, nothing was sure.

The campus's cramped roads had become black with night, and the sudden right angles made her headlights almost useless as she drove to the hospital. What Haley said couldn't be true. Meg hadn't done those things. How could she? It had been Austin.

Confusion-born tears started, and the car threatened to stall as she took a corner too tight.

Austin had been there. Haley was lying. She was a mean, spiteful bitch who'd pretended to like her for her own sadistic mind games. Meg should've known it was too good to be true that Haley actually *liked* her. People as perfect as Haley didn't make friends with basket cases like her. Rorry was even worse, pretending to protect her from

Austin when all Rorry was doing was protecting Haley's "investment."

"I'm a plaything to them. A toy." Wiping her eyes, she bounced over the road bumps, struggling not to cry from the heartache of being used. "I can't believe I painted a picture for him. Son of a bitch. Son of a bitch!"

The canvas was beside her where Austin once sat, its lines lost in the darkness. Throwing it away wasn't an option. It was her best work, the beginning of something totally new, and now, she'd think of him every time she looked at it.

"Damn him. Damn them both," she whispered. Frustrated, Meg hit the dash, and her hand began to bleed again through the bandage. Meg stared at the slick sheen leaking out, her panic rising anew. Was it really bleeding or just an illusion? Had she cut her hand or burned it?

"I hate this car," she said softly, and then louder, when she realized she'd missed the turn and was headed into the nearby park, "I hate this car! Why am I even driving this car!"

Suddenly her headlights gleamed on the ragged silhouette of a man in the road, waving at her to stop. It was Christopher, and gasping, Meg spun the wheel to avoid him. That damned little dog of his jerked his lead free and ran away, but Christopher froze in fear. Panicking, Meg hit the gas instead of the brake.

With a sickening lurch, the car angled off the road and onto the open grass toward the trees. Meg shrieked, paralyzed as the memory of her accident rose up, thick and smothering. The impact of the curb bounced her head into the wheel, and dazed, she could do nothing but cross her arms over her face as the trees flashed past bright with light. With a jaw-snapping thud, the car ran into a tree and stalled.

For three seconds, Meg didn't move, her breath a harsh rasp as she remembered where she was. There'd been no airbag to cushion her this time, and the taste of blood slicked her teeth. Dazed, she looked at the empty seat beside her, relief pushing out the fear. It wasn't one of her nightmares. It was real and she was okay. Austin wasn't here, his hand mangled and his leg nearly severed at the hip by a metal fence support. There was only a canvas lying on the floor, one that would haunt her for the rest of her life.

"I hate this car," she whispered, wishing she'd gotten the airbag replaced along with the passenger side door. But it hadn't seemed to matter if she wasn't going to drive the thing.

Then Christopher banged on the window, and she jumped, shrieking.

"You have to kill them!" he shouted through the window, and Meg scrambled to the other side of the car and got out in a panic.

"Stay away from me!" she exclaimed as she reached back in for her purse, backing away from him as he came around the car. "You're crazy. Crazy!"

"Like hell I am," he growled, and she gasped as he grabbed her arm. "It's not too late. Come with me to the fountain. They need moving water. That's how they get here. They haven't left. Help me. We have to kill them both or you'll never know what's real again. Don't let them take you. Perfection isn't real. *They* aren't real!"

If they aren't real, then why do you want to kill them? she thought, but there was no logic to crazy. "Get away from me!" Meg wedged his hand off her. Shoving him back, she began to run to the hospital. She had to talk to Dr. Jillium, stand in front of her and find out what was real and what wasn't, because if Perfection wasn't an illusion, than what she'd done wasn't either.

Breathless, Meg reached the outskirts of the parking lot, turning to look behind her at the shadows as she found herself under the brighter lights. Christopher wasn't following, and she forced herself to slow, tugging her skirt straight and clutching her purse as she paced between the cars, trying to hide her limp as she angled for the main entrance. Her hand throbbed, and she held it to her middle, hiding it. It was after visiting hours, but if she could slip past the lobby desk, she should be fine.

The flash of headlights from a slow-moving car arched toward her, and she ducked down behind a parked truck, not sure why except that Haley seemed to think she'd set fire to Dr. Jillium's office, and fear and uncertainty had begun to gnaw at her. Unmoving, she watched Daniel park his black sedan, the door echoing as he slammed it shut and headed for the entrance.

Meg's pulse raced. He was going to talk to Dr. Jillium. Why else would he be here? Hunched and hurting, Meg stood to follow. Her lip was swollen, and an instinctive lick brought her up short at the unexpected taste of blood. She froze and looked down at herself. She was a mess.

Exhaling, Meg forced herself to ease her death-grip on her purse. She used her sleeve to wipe the streaks of tears from her face, then fingercombed her hair and slapped the dirt from her dress. Squaring her shoulders, she risked a quick look behind her to make sure Christopher was gone before slipping in through the wide glass doors to follow Daniel.

"Third floor," the receptionist was saying to the confident man flashing his badge, and Meg ducked out of sight. Stomach cramping, she watched Daniel give the woman a pleasant, flirtatious salute before heading for the elevator, his hands in his pockets and his steps jaunty. Drawing back, Meg headed to the stairs.

The door was heavy, and she pushed it aside just enough to slip past. Knees watery, she took the stairs fast, her hip throbbing and her breath heavy by the time she reached the third floor. Breath rasping, she cautiously looked out of the long, narrow window onto the hallway, bright under the fluorescent lights.

Kim Harrison

Meg's shoulders eased. A floor polisher hummed, the operator wearing ear buds, his back to her as he moved his machine in time with unheard music. The woman manning the desk was busy with work, but she looked up when the elevator dinged and Daniel stepped out, all smiles as he draped himself over the high counter and charmed Dr. Jillium's room number from her with a flash of smiling teeth and his badge.

The woman pointed down the hall toward Meg, and she drew back from the window, pulse hammering. She waited, her back to the wall, until Daniel's steps passed her. Haley knew too much to not be working with Dr. Jillium, but why? Why would she say such things?

Unless it was true....

Meg wiped her palms on her pants. The nurse had her head down and the floor cleaner was dancing his machine the other way. Purse held tight, she eased into the hallway, glancing at the desk before following Daniel once down the night-emptied corridor. She breathed easier after turning the corner, just in time to see the furl of Daniel's suit coat slip past a closing door.

Meg ran to catch up, wedging her fingers between the heavy door and the frame before it shut.

"Daniel," Dr. Jillium said, her voice both anxious and relieved. "Tell me you found her."

"She's not at her apartment." Daniel's low voice was harder to hear, and Meg pressed closer.

"Did you check her old one?" Dr. Jillium asked.

"I looked at both. There's no sign of Chris, either. Are you going to eat that?"

"Be my guest." Dr. Jillium's tone was sour, and Meg heard the faint clink of a spoon. "I really messed this up. She was doing so well. The Fitrecepon was working. It was working, Daniel. She wasn't hurting anyone, and she was making more progress there in her fantasy than she would with any amount of truth in a facility."

Fantasy? Meg thought, confusion spilling through her. Maybe Christopher was right. Maybe Haley and Rorry were the delusions, lying to her about Austin. *Can you see them? Can you see them yet?* Head down, Meg looked in her purse, pushing past her phone and diary to the smoke-stained vials of Fitrecepon. How could she be having a bad reaction if she was better?

"I'm not arguing that it's working," Daniel said, the clink of the spoon a sharp punctuation. "But explain to me how she skipped the initial warnings and went right into overdose."

"I don't know." Dr. Jillium sighed, and Meg shifted her weight to her other foot, her hip aching. "Maybe I wasn't listening. Damn it, Daniel, she was doing better. Real progress."

"Have you given your statement yet?" he asked, and Meg's brow furrowed.

Dr. Jillium made a soft noise of negation. "About the fire? No. What did Meg say?"

"Worried about losing your license? You should be," he said in a sing-song tone.

"What did she say, Daniel?"

"It's on the news," he said, and there was the clink of a dish being set down. "Where's your remote? I'll find it for you."

"What. Did. She. Say," Dr. Jillium intoned, and Daniel sighed.

"That Austin came in a jealous rage, knocked you out, set fire to your office to destroy Meg's access to Fitrecepon."

"Damn," Dr. Jillium said softly, or maybe Meg just imagined it. Her grip on her purse began to tighten as a confusion-born anger seeped into her.

"They're going to find out, Janice. Meg is going to find out."

With a decisive motion, Meg stiff-armed the door open and walked in, her steps not as graceful as she wanted because of the pain. "Find out what?" she asked.

Daniel bolted to his feet from where he had been half sitting against the cupboards that lined the wall opposite the bed, his shock obvious in his wide-eyed expression. Dr. Jillium was sitting up in bed, looking odd in a paisley-blue smock. She looked older without makeup, her eyes tired but quickly losing her surprise. A deep sadness took its place, as she slumped against the headboard, her pillow lost behind her.

But her brow furrowed when Daniel reached behind himself for his cuffs. "Daniel, I swear, if you cuff another one of my clients, I will turn you in myself. Meg is not a criminal."

Daniel's eyes narrowed as he settled back. "I am failing to see the difference," he muttered.

Turn him in? For what? Meg wondered, her anger making her shoulders stiff.

"Come on in, Meg," Dr. Jillium said with a small gesture. "I'm glad you're here. I have a few things to talk to you about."

Meg's lips pressed together. "Not with him in the room," she said, and Daniel, flipped his suit coat aside to show off his snapped holster.

"Really, Daniel?" Dr. Jillium said with a tired sigh, and he frowned at both of them.

"I'll be right outside," he said as he grabbed the back of a rolling chair. Meg warily sidestepped out of his way. "I'm sorry, Doctor. You know as well as I where this is going."

Meg stiffened at the treat, saying nothing as he dragged the rolling chair out into the hall. His head was down over his phone as the door shut, and her worry deepened. But she needed answers.

Kim Harrison

"What am I going to figure out?" Meg asked again, and Dr. Jillium winced. "That Fitrecepon is dangerous? That you made me worse, not better? That like the Titanic, I'm two thousand feet in the air and sinking?" she added, flinging a hand uselessly into the air. It was the one bandaged and bloodied, and she hid it behind her. "I'm seeing things that aren't there. I'm hearing things no one else does. I was better off living in that dark apartment."

"That's not true." Dr. Jillium winced. "Look at you."

"I am *hallucinating*, Dr. J," she said, pacing. "I just had a conversation with two people I'm having serious doubts exist. They knew all about you. All about me. They were trying to get me to believe that Austin has been dead for the last three years. You can't tell me that's not a hallucination."

Dr. Jillium said nothing, her sorrowful eyes fixed on Meg.

Meg felt her face go cold. "Dr. Jillium?" she questioned, no longer sure she had the right to be angry.

"I'm sorry, Meg," the woman said softly. "I don't know what went wrong. Maybe I shouldn't have let you maintain your fantasy, but you weren't showing any sign of complications. You made so much progress in the last few days, I suppose I blinded myself to them. You even made the conscious decision to leave Austin. I was so proud of you. I thought that perhaps you were finally ready to accept what had happened and move on," she said, her smile both sad and proud.

Breathless, Meg felt for the chair, fingers fumbling. "Accept what? What happened?"

Dr. Jillium gestured helplessly. "Austin died in that car accident three years ago."

Meg sat down hard. That was it. She was crazy. Not just crazy, but bat-shit crazy.

"He can't be dead," Meg said, her voice breathy as she tried to make sense of it. "You told me you talked to him," she accused. "How could he be dead if you told me you talked to him? Were you making a fool of me just to get your pills on the market?"

"No!" Dr. Jillium protested, her eyes going wide in a guilty protest. "It wasn't like that at all. You were making more progress thinking he was real than when you knew he wasn't, and I didn't see the harm. Meg, I'm so sorry," Dr. Jillium pleaded, but Meg hardly heard, her mind trying to wrap itself around the alternate truths as a crushing loss rose up, as fresh and biting as it had been three years ago. Austin was dead, and she had killed him. She had killed him trying to feel something.

"I'm so sorry to be doing this from a hospital room," Dr. Jillium was saying. "Fitrecepon was designed to bring your emotions closer to the surface so you could deal with the grief and find closure. It seemed to be working. You'd stabilized," she said as if trying to convince herself. "Realized his memory was holding you back. Took steps to leave him behind. That a part of you would rebel and fight to retain your delusion was unexpected."

Breathless, Meg tried to understand. It had been *her* who had knocked Dr. Jillium out and set fire to the building? Dizzy, Meg looked at her bandaged hand and the blood leaking through. It was cut, not burned. *How could I remember it the other way?*

"I don't blame you for any of it," Dr. Jillium said as Meg hid her hand.

"I don't understand," Meg whispered. "How can Austin be dead? Who have I been having dinner with every night?" She looked up as Dr. Jillium reached for her hand. "Who has been driving me around?"

"You have," she said as she gave Meg's hand a squeeze. "It was easier for you to remember it as Austin being there, him driving instead of you. Meg, it's okay," she said when Meg groaned at the unreal travesty of it all, the fool she had been. "You're making progress. You wouldn't even get into a car a year ago."

My God, everyone on campus must think I'm crazy, talking to myself for three years when I thought I was talking to Austin, Meg thought in despair, and then her jaw tightened. Dr. Jillium had let her run around campus making a fool of herself? Talking to no one? No wonder she didn't have any real friends.

"Look at your hand, Meg," Dr. Jillium said, mistaking her anger for disbelief. "You told the police that you burned it, but it's cut from breaking the glass. Look at it. Look at it! You are having an extreme reaction to the Fitrecepon. I have to take you off it, but we'll get through this together. I promise."

I can't deal with this, Meg thought suddenly, her stomach knotting as her fingers felt a slick smoothness of the blood leaking out of her bandage. Haley had told her the truth, and she had just walked out on her.

And then Meg's breath caught. If Haley wasn't an illusion, then Perfection wasn't either. It was real. "And my new friends?" she asked, her voice sounding as if coming from someone else.

"I'm afraid they're new imaginary surrogates for Austin, created to cushion your psyche as you let him go," Dr. Jillium said.

Meg stood, her arms over her middle as she turned her back on her. *"I will not throw my chance at utopia away because I'm scared to believe in it."*

"I didn't see any harm in it as you gave them a semester's lifespan. I'm sorry, Meg," Dr. Jillium said gently. "I've seen this before. I'm going to have to take you off the Fitrecepon before the changes become permanent. "

Her back to Dr. Jillium, Meg clenched her purse closer. "Haley and Rorry are not imaginary," she said. "We went shopping. I stayed at her apartment. I helped her pick it out and everything in it."

Kim Harrison

"You picked it out, Meg," Dr. Jillium insisted. "To get away from Austin's memory. You did it, and it's okay. You just need to do it on your own, now. I won't press charges, and it will be almost as if it never happened. We can work this out. I won't leave you. We can do it together."

Meg spun back, feeling unreal and light. "Work this out?" she said, knowing that there would be no jail, but rather a nice comfortable room at the nearest mental facility. Probably right next to Christopher. "They are *not* imaginary," she insisted, refusing to let Dr. Jillium take them away along with Austin. "We played putt-putt. I have the score card."

"Meg…"

"No, look. See?" Head down Meg dug through her purse past her diary to find it. It had been a beautiful evening, the first in a long time that she'd felt free, and she wouldn't let her therapist tell her it had all been in her head. "Look at it!" Meg demanded, her hand shaking as she held it out, recalling how Rorry had faked his totals and Haley had gotten a hole in one.

Dr. Jillium took it. "This is your handwriting," the older woman said, and Meg snatched it back, staring at the tight, cramped writing that was clearly not her own.

"It is not," she said flatly, startled when Dr. Jillium reached into her purse for her diary and flipped it open. Meg's lips parted at page after page of that same cramped writing. *It was empty. It had been empty!*

Perfunctory **Af**fection

"That's not mine..." Meg said, panic bubbling up, black and thick to swamp her as she grabbed it and read a passage she didn't remember writing, about her going shopping for the first time in a month, buying things to outfit her new apartment that she'd just picked out, getting her hair cut and a manicure—all on her own. "This wasn't me," she said, head shaking. "Haley or Rorry must have done it. They're trying to trick me. I don't know why. I want to go. I want to!" she pleaded.

Dr. Jillium took the diary and closed it. "Think about it, Meg. What's the most logical explanation? I have two years of your diaries in my office. Or I did," she finished sourly. "All of them written in the same handwriting."

Conveniently burned to nothing, Meg thought.

"I'm sorry, Meg, but I can't let you stay on the Fitrecepon."

Meg's head snapped up. *I can handle Perfection. I'm not going to give it up*, she thought as she backed to the door. "I have to go. I have to talk to Haley."

"Haley isn't real." Dr. Jillium flung the covers off her feet, then hung her head, breathing hard. "She's a side effect of an overdose of Fitrecepon," she said faintly, and then louder, "*Daniel?*"

Feeling trapped, Meg looked at the door as Daniel came in. Seeing Dr. Jillium's heartache and Meg's determination, his expression hardened.

Kim Harrison

It might be Meg's handwriting in page after page of that diary, but Haley and Rorry were real. Perfection was a place. Christopher was right, and she suddenly wanted to go there. There was nowhere else she could escape the reality that she had killed Austin and lied to herself for the last three years.

"I don't believe you," Meg said, voice quavering as she warned Daniel off with an outstretched hand. "I don't believe you! Get out of my way."

But Dr. Jillium had swung her feet to the floor, sitting on the edge of the bed as she caught her balance. "I'm sorry, Meg. I really am. This is my failing, not yours. But we'll get you better."

But I don't want to be better. It might be Dr. Jillium's failing, but Meg would be the one who'd land in a medical facility. *Like Christopher,* she thought, tensing.

Christopher. He was going to go to the fountain and try to kill them. If she saved them, maybe they would take her. Wouldn't that make up for torching Dr. Jillium's office?

"Okay, Meg. Nice and easy," Daniel said as he warily approached, not trusting her silent stance. "I won't cuff you if you don't make me."

She nodded, her fist clenching into a hard knot. "I won't give you any trouble," she lied.

Dr. Jillium's eyes narrowed. "Daniel..." she warned, but it was too late, and when Daniel reached for her, Meg lashed out, shoving him into the cabinet. He hit with a thud, swearing as he went down. Meg shrieked as she sprang over his feet and hit the door, running for the parking lot.

She wanted to go to Perfection. Haley was real. She'd said the Fitrecepon let Meg see them. Maybe with enough pills, the way would open and she could go. *I've seen it. I've painted it. It exists.*

For as Meg saw it, it was better to be delusional and a slave living with the fey than sane and responsible for Austin's death.

Nineteen

She couldn't stomach getting into her car even if it wasn't smashed into a park tree; the memory of Austin dying beside her was as fresh as if it had just happened. And so Meg ran to the fountain, her sore ankle and new sandals making her awkward as she shifted from lawn to curb to pavement, making a raven's path to the center of the campus.

The quad was empty, and lungs heaving, Meg slid to an exhausted halt at the edge of the trees to wait for Haley and Rorry. Her chest hurt as she fought for breath, grief and anger making her confused. Slowly she pulled herself upright as she stared at the brightly lit fountain. The chattering water was an odd, Coke-bottle green in the underwater lights. She'd either missed them or they weren't here yet. Limbs feeling like rags, she scuffed to the fountain, fearing the worst. Christopher had said he was going to kill them.

Kim Harrison

But the fountain was empty of everything but a frog hanging in a still point in the moving water. Moths beat about the lights shining on the angel pouring out her vial, and spiders had made glistening webs to catch them.

"I'm going crazy," Meg whispered as she sat on the edge, her back going cool from the intermittent spray. Christopher had said they needed moving water to get to Perfection and back. Where were they?

"Haley?" she called, getting no answer. "Rorry, are you out here? I just want to talk." It was just what Austin had said.

Austin is dead, she reminded herself.

Emotion washed through her, and she shoved it back down where she could ignore it. If she could get to Perfection, what had happened with Austin wouldn't matter. Flustered, she smoothed her hair and ran a nervous hand down her skirt.

The pills, she thought suddenly, swinging her purse forward and rummaging until she found a vial. Pulse fast, she shook a handful into her hand and swallowed them dry. "Haley?" she called as she stood up. Maybe Christopher had scared them off. Or they had left already. Where else was there running water? *Putt-putt?* Meg thought, anxious as she paced around the fountain in search of any sign they'd been and gone.

And then she stopped stock-still upon seeing Rorry and Haley in the shadows just under the ancient oak trees. *Why didn't she answer?* Meg thought, afraid to move. Dr. Jillium was wrong. They were real. Maybe she'd written all that in her diary, but they were real.

"I just want to talk," Meg whispered. "Please."

Lips pressed, Haley came forward looking as perfect as always. "Why are you here?" she asked, and Meg warmed at the annoyance in her voice.

"I want to go," she said, and Rorry, now two steps behind her, winced. "Please. I'll do anything," Meg begged. "Don't leave me here. I've got nothing left. You were right. Austin is dead. I did those things, but I didn't mean to, and now I know. It won't happen again. Please, I can't stay here."

"Haley..." Rorry coaxed, and Meg's hope soared when the angry slant to Haley's brow eased as she arranged Meg's hair about her ears.

"I wish I could," the smaller woman said. "It's not my decision anymore. When you tried to kill Dr. Jillium to find Perfection, you proved you weren't deserving of it."

Meg stiffened as she felt everything slip away. "But I didn't kill her. I pulled her to safety," she protested. "I know Austin wasn't really there. It was me, and I'm sorry. I won't do it again."

But Haley only smiled sadly, her cool fingers dropping to arrange the collar of Meg's sundress. "They can't see the difference. If it were up to me, I'd say yes, but you're too damaged for Perfection." Meg couldn't move as Haley tugged her close, giving her what felt like a good-bye hug.

"I'm so sorry," Haley whispered, her breath shifting the hair beside Meg's ear. "You would have liked it there, and you are so talented that I might never have had to come back here for years and years. I wish it could be so. I wish you hadn't come here. This is hard."

Meg stumbled when Haley let go and stepped back, that same regretful, fond expression on her face. Rorry was looking nervous, his attention alternating between them and the fountain. "Please," Meg begged, her skin beginning to tingle as the moths beat faster against the lights. "I can be perfect. I have two vials of Fitrecepon. See?"

She fumbled for them, holding them out like an offering, but Haley only closed Meg's hands over them to hide them. "No. You might have been, but you aren't. I'm sorry."

Anger flared in Meg. It was Austin's fault. It was always Austin's fault, even when he had been dead for three years.

Behind her, Rorry tucked his phone away. "Haley? It's time."

"Stay here," Haley said, her hand raised as if she was telling a dog to go home. Turning, she moved to join Rorry. "Don't try to follow us. You won't be able to, and you'll only make it harder for us to go."

"Christopher!" Meg shouted, desperate to keep them from leaving. "He wants to kill you. He told me he was going to try to kill you!"

Perfunctory **Affection**

Haley's expression blanked. "Does he know how to get through the veil?" she asked, and from the darkness behind her, Meg heard an angry shout.

"You little bitch!" Christopher yelled, and Meg spun, gasping as Christopher raced out of the dark toward them. His hands were clenched and a frighteningly intent expression pinched his eyes, turning his expression ugly. His dog was at his heels, barking furiously.

"Go." Rorry's face was white as he pushed Haley behind him. "Go now!"

"Stop!" Meg shouted. She lurched to get between Christopher and them, then shrieked as Christopher shoved her aside. There was a knife in his grip. Eyes wild, Christopher swung it at Rorry, spittle flying from his lips as he howled like a mad thing.

"I won't go back! You're all insane! I'll kill you all if I have to!"

Haley darted back leaving Rorry to dodge Christopher's wild swings. An odd smile played about Rorry's lips as he shifted and spun, and Meg caught her breath, wondering if they would make it after all.

But then that little dog darted in, fixing his teeth into Rorry's pant leg. Arms waving, Rorry tripped, going down to narrowly miss Christopher's knife swinging over his head. The dog yelped and ran for the shadows as Rorry rolled, trying to stay out of the way.

"Christopher, stop it!" Meg cried out as she grabbed his arm yanking him back to give Rorry time to get to his feet. Shaken but unharmed, Rorry spun upright, his feet just shy of the fountain's drifting spray.

"What are you doing!" Christopher shouted, his arms waving wildly. "They have to die! We'll never know what is real and what isn't if they are alive."

But Meg stood in front of him, refusing to back down. "I'm not letting you hurt them," she said, voice quavering. "Go away."

"I'm trying to save your sanity," Christopher said, and then his eyes flicked behind her, his face going ashen.

"Maybe I don't want to be sane," Meg said.

But Christopher was silent, his gaze fixed behind her. Turning, she froze, shocked at the shimmering haze now spreading within the spray of the fountain. Haley stood in it, her form indistinct. Meg's breath came in slow, and she pulled herself up. The ocean was black with dusk, but the mountains behind Haley still held the red of the sun. It was Perfection.

"Rorry!" Haley shouted, reaching for him. "It's closing! Hurry! You don't have a talisman!"

Face white, Rorry dove for the wet pavement.

"No-o-o-o!" Christopher bellowed, and Meg spun.

But Christopher hadn't moved, his ragged clothes furling as he flung his hand at Rorry. Meg caught her breath thinking it was that knife, but it was only a weighted bola, glittering like silver as it spun through the air and tangled about Rorry's feet, even as he slid into the spray.

"Take my hand!" Haley called as she reached for him, but her hand passed right through as if he was no longer real. For an instant, she stared, shocked, and then realized what had happened. "Your feet! It's silver!"

But it was too late, and as Rorry frantically disentangled the frail length of silver and threw it from him, the glittering glow on the mountains behind Haley dulled and vanished taking Haley and the vision of Perfection with her.

"Haley..." Rorry whispered, a look of disbelief widening his eyes as he sat alone in the wet spray. From the fountain, a frog trilled, and was silent.

"Let's see how you like my new game," Christopher muttered.

Meg jerked, the image of what she might have had still burning in her mind as she turned to Christopher now pacing toward Rorry, that knife again in his hands. "Run!" she cried as she grabbed Christopher's arm. "Rorry, run!"

"Let go of me, you fool!" Christopher lashed out with his knife.

White-hot pain struck through Meg, and her grip sprang away. Expression ugly, Christopher turned to Rorry, the bewildered man still struggling to his feet. He was helpless, and Meg jumped at Christopher, determined to bring him down.

Kim Harrison

Christopher grunted in surprise as she hit, and they went down as a flash of light blinded them.

"Go! Run!" Meg shouted as she grappled with Christopher, struggling as he shoved her off him and tried to stand. Hands aching and slippery from blood, she grabbed his leg, eyes squinted shut as Christopher fought to be free of her. Her only goal was to give Rorry time to step through the light. Christopher's foot hit her face, and she gasped, almost letting go as pain shocked through her. Eyes clenched shut, she hung on, crying through the tears of pain.

"I won't let you. I won't let you!" she shouted, unable to see, and then she screamed as someone took her around the waist and yanked her from Christopher.

"He's trying to kill them!" she exclaimed, fighting to be free. "He's got a knife!"

"Whoa, whoa, whoa! Easy there, Meg. We've got Chris," a familiar voice called out, and Meg went limp, crying through the blood still dripping down her face from her nose. It was Daniel. The bright light hadn't been the veil opening, but the cops.

Wiping her face, Meg looked at the empty spray, then lifted her gaze to the surrounding lights and milling officers. Rorry and Haley were gone, and her heartache thundered down. They had gone and left her in this wretched world where nothing was perfect and everything was wrong. She'd never find it again. "Let me go. Let me go!" she demanded, but they wouldn't, and it was too late even if they did. There was no glow in the spray, no veil made real by mist and dusk. It was just wet cement.

Did he make it? she wondered, not seeing Rorry, but she was pretty sure he hadn't. Meg hung her head, knowing the loss he was feeling, the ache to have been left behind, the knowledge that the wait would be like forever.

"Put her in the car. Gently," Daniel admonished. "She's ill, not crazy."

Meg stared blankly at him, wondering if he knew if Haley and Rorry were real or not. Christopher was facedown on the sidewalk, his knife being admired by two other officers as three more roughly searched him for anything else. The man wouldn't shut up, his demands that they let him kill them bouncing off the nearby buildings and bringing students to the windows.

Numb, Meg held her injured arm. The silver bola that had tangled Rorry was in Daniel's hands. The detective held it as if it had no meaning, but Meg knew it had been why Rorry couldn't make it through the veil. No wonder cuffs were made of steel.

"They have to die!" Christopher shouted when they pulled him up, his voice echoing through the quad. "Perfection isn't real! It's a lie! You have to let me kill them before they come back for all of you!"

"This way, ma'am." A cop was holding out a hand to help her up, and her resolve strengthened as she found her feet. "Watch your head," he added when they got to the waiting car, and Meg obediently went into the back of the cruiser. The thump of the door shutting made her jump, and she wiped her eyes, scanning the shadows for a glimpse of Rorry.

She would get to Perfection. She'd risked her life to save Rorry's, and that had to count for something. She wouldn't forget. She couldn't, now that she'd seen it. She'd give up everything to go there, even her sanity.

Twenty

om was crying again as he stumbled through his usual litany, his raw emotions that once bothered Meg now a background of white noise as she sat in one of the smaller common rooms and tried to keep track of the conversation enough to answer intelligently if the therapist asked her something. There was an art to it, but Meg had had a few weeks to practice. Her jeans and colorful top were a sad attempt at giving the "clients" a feeling of normalcy. But they all knew they were trapped behind doors that opened only one way unless you had the right card. The bars were made of sedatives and "behavioral modifiers" and came in little paper cups and syringes.

Grimacing, Meg rubbed a new scuff off her sandals. They were the ones that she'd bought with Haley. There was a clear nip in the air and the leaves were changing, but she had refused to wear anything else. The sneakers she'd been given to wear made her look like a dork.

Kim Harrison

"Meg?"

Startled, Meg let her foot drop. "Yes?"

Simon was looking at her, the therapist's over-eager demeanor making him stand out more than his name tag and ID lanyard. Elana, who'd accidently left her kid in a hot car to die, was staring at the floor, lost in a memory. Laura, unable to handle having burned down her house and everyone in it with a lit cigarette, was totally in la-la land. Meg didn't know why Karl was here, yet, his eyes glassy from too much sedative. He'd only been coming for a week and was still in slippers. He had a definite aversion to anything sharp, though.

"I was wondering if you would like to add anything to the conversation?" Simon asked, and Karl made an odd, gasping gurgle before slumping back into his haze.

Meg shifted uneasily, having no idea what they'd been talking about. The drugs Dr. Jillium had her on made her short-term memory shit. "Ah…"

Simon smiled patiently, but Meg could see his frustration under it. "Tom was explaining how he can still sometimes hear his wife's voice, or the shower running in the morning, and how that gives him both comfort and guilt."

"Sure." Meg sat up straighter, her gaze going out of the wide, double-pained windows to the facility's peaceful, pastoral grounds. "I can understand that. That's why I spent three years imagining that Austin was alive."

Perfunctory
A**ffection**

"And now you realize how damaging that was," Simon prompted, his voice giving away how his exasperation obvious he was to be going over things that they'd discussed before. No one made fast progress in group therapy. It was a place to start and end, not unload the real dirt that they were all buried under.

"In the long, run, sure." Meg's gaze strayed to the shallow pond and the surrounding trees. By rights, she should be sitting there at the white bench with Dr. Jillium for her daily chat, but Dr. Jillium hadn't shown this morning, and so she was here in group therapy.

"And Rorry and Haley?" Simon insisted, and Meg mentally rolled her eyes.

"Were invented to take his place when I began to break away from the delusion," Meg said to give him a thrill.

"Very good. Tom, do you have anything to build on that?" the ham-handed therapist said, clearly relieved, and Meg smiled, her gaze still out the window as Rorry stepped out from under the trees. Her smile widened as the lanky man settled himself on the bench beside the pond as if to wait for her, his long legs stretched out almost all the way across the crushed gravel walk and into the grass. Christopher's ratty dog was with him. The two had apparently made friends now that Christopher was imprisoned behind paper cups and white walls as well.

Meg sighed, wondering if Rorry could see her through the wire-lined windows. They were both trapped, her in a drug-laced prison, and he in her reality. Why someone hadn't come back to rescue him gave her hope. Maybe they were waiting for her.

The creak of the door to the hall pulled Meg's attention up and away, relief filling her when she realized it was Dr. Jillium.

"Excuse me, Simon," the woman said with a smile. "Meg, I'm sorry I'm late. Would you like to stay and finish your session or continue on with me?"

Immediately Meg stood, her pace fast as she headed for the door and a few moments of escape.

Laura pulled herself out of her funk, her expression cross. "How come she gets to leave and the rest of us have to sit here listening to Tom whine about his dead wife again?"

"Laura!" Simon admonished, and Dr. Jillium dropped back into the hallway to hide the hint of a smile. "That is totally out of line."

"I'm not the one hogging the entire hour with the same old crap he's been talking about for the last two years," Laura accused, and Meg slipped into the hall, shutting the door firmly behind her.

"Thank you," Meg said with a grateful sigh. "I thought you weren't coming today. Simon has about as much finesse as a black Lab."

"Which has its uses." Dr. Jillium matched Meg's slow step as they headed down the hall. Behind them, Tom was screaming at Laura. Two orderlies had gone in, and Meg was doubly glad to have made an escape. She didn't need to be a part of anyone's breakthrough.

"I'm, ah, sorry for being late," Dr. Jillium said as she ran her card and they went into a less institutional looking wing. There was carpet on the floor, and the windows opened. "I had an unexpected errand. Do you want to take our usual walk?"

Meg thought about Rorry outside. Dr. Jillium wouldn't see him, but she might see the dog. "No. It's kind of chilly today. Can we talk in your office?"

"Sure." Dr. Jillium nodded at the orderly sitting at the nearby desk, and they continued on into the office area. "I've got something there to show you, anyway. How was your day yesterday?"

Meg's shoulders eased even more. The farther they were from cold white tile and harsh white light, the better she felt. "Fine. Thank you for the access to my paint and canvas."

"My pleasure. Do you need anything else?"

Meg winced, already knowing the answer. "Better light?"

Dr. Jillium smiled. "I'll see what I can do."

"Um, how's Christopher doing?" Meg asked. She'd heard him in the night last week, but he hadn't been in the cafeteria even once.

"Meg, you know I can't talk about my other patients." Meg gave her a sidelong look, and Dr. Jillium sighed.

"Not good. He's still fixed on the belief that your Rorry and Haley are the same two figures that featured in his delusion."

"Mmmm." Meg's steps were soft on the carpet, and the real wood trim was comforting. She ran a hand down it as they walked, enjoying the smooth feel.

"I was hoping that he could join the group by now, but I'm concerned that seeing you would only reinforce his beliefs."

Meg nodded. "It's hard being cooped up all day."

"I know, and I'm sorry," Dr. Jillium said as they turned the corner. There was an orderly break room halfway down the hall, and Meg's pulse quickened. The guards were never far away. "I'm hoping that I can increase your privileges this week," Dr. Jillium said as they reached her office and she gestured for Meg to go in. "You've made a lot of progress. That you freely admit that Rorry and Haley were constructs to ease the loss of Austin was a big step."

But Meg hardly heard. She stood, frozen three steps into Dr. Jillium's office. Her painting, the one she'd made for Rorry, was sitting propped up in one of the office chairs facing the desk. A sudden sweat made her feel both hot and cold. It was Perfection, the light of sunset still shining on the hills and the veil between their realities, the thinnest.

"Meg?" Dr. Jillium prompted, and Meg took a gasping breath.

"W-where," she croaked out, her voice harsh.

Dr. Jillium went to the canvas, hoisting it up as if it was just a picture. "It was in your car," she said, smiling as her eyes appreciatively traced the lines. "I was finally able to get it when they auctioned it off this morning. I thought you might want it. Seeing as you're painting again."

Meg forced her arms down from around her waist, fear creeping out from the dark places in her soul. "No," she whispered, and Dr. Jillium turned, a tight, knowing expression in her eyes. "I don't want it," Meg said forcefully. "You can have it."

Dr. Jillium set the canvas down, her motions slow in regret. "They're not real, Meg. I know they feel as if they are, but they aren't."

"They are!" Meg shouted, then turned away, hands on her head as she wished she could take it back. "Rorry is out there right now," she said softly, unable to stop herself. "Why should I wallow in lies? I'm not the one having trouble with the truth. I saw him this morning. He's there with Christopher's old dog."

Dr. Jillium turned to her window, set to look out over the parking lot. "I don't see them."

"He's not in the parking lot," Meg said as if Dr. Jillium was being stupid, then lowered her voice. "He was at the lake. It's the frogs and spiders," she said, knowing how foolish that sounded but unable to stop herself. "I can't tell if he

Kim Harrison

attracts them, or if he just likes the same things they do. I think he's waiting for me."

Dr. Jillium went to stand behind her desk. "I'm sorry, Meg. I want to increase your meds this week."

Anger flared, and Meg forced her hands to unclench. "I don't need more meds," she said softly. "I need to get out of here. He's waiting for me. I saved him, and they changed their minds. They want me to go. They'll let me in, and you have no right to keep me here."

"Meg, why don't you sit down."

"Why? I'm not being unreasonable," Meg said, and Dr. Jillium's lips pressed. "I just want to leave. I'm a prisoner here, and you know it!" The last was a shout, and Meg held up a hand in apology. "Sorry, sorry," she said, but Dr. Jillium was already reaching for the desk intercom.

"Chuck? Can you come in here for a moment?" she said as she thumbed the button.

"Chuck? Really?" Meg said bitterly, knowing all the really good orderlies on a first-name basis. "I'm not losing it, Dr. J. I'm as sane as you. The Fitrecepon changed how I see things. That's what it's supposed to do, and you want to increase my sedation? Make me a drooling idiot so *you* don't have to face reality? I know what's real. I've *seen* it! It's out there!"

The door opened, and Meg turned as the large black man came in, his white orderly uniform hiding a syringe somewhere. "Hi, Meg."

Perfunctory **Af**fection

"You stay out of this, Chuck," Meg warned, a hand raised as she backed to the windows.

"I'm trying to help you," Dr. Jillium said, but it was clearly a ploy to distract her, and Meg didn't take her eyes off Chuck.

"Come on, Meg," the large man said soothingly. "Don't make me stick you."

Meg kept backing up, wishing the windows were open. "Try it," she threatened, her eyes going to Dr. Jillium. "I dare you to try the Fitrecepon yourself, Dr. J," she said. "You'll see them too. And then you'll have to believe in Perfection and let me out." Her back hit the corner, and she felt the bookcase, not daring to throw a volume at Chuck. He was that big. "I saved Rorry. They'll let me in now. They want me!"

Chuck moved at her last panicked outcry, and Meg lurched to get away, shrieking as he snagged her easily. "They're out there!" she shouted as he spun her into a submission hold. "I've seen them!" she added as he yanked the top off his syringe, and then she yelped as he jammed it into her. "Damn you, Chuck!" she swore. "I'm not crazy!"

"I know you aren't Miss Meg," he said in his slow drawl, and Meg slumped as everything seemed to go warm and soft. The meds were taking hold, dampening her, making nothing seem important.

"I'm not crazy," she said, hearing her words begin to slur as her strength left her and she sagged in Chuck's arms. "You think I'm crazy, but they are there. An entire world of them. Take the Fitrecepon, Dr. J. Try it." Exhaling, Meg closed her eyes, her last image of her canvas. "And then you'll have to believe in Perfection."

Slumping in Chuck's grip, Meg went silent, grateful that the drugs had relieved her of the onus of telling the truth. "She's down," she heard Chuck say, and then she felt herself lifted, cradled in his thick, beefy arms to be carried back to her room. She'd be lucky now if she got out into the garden again by spring. *Son of a bitch…*

"Thank you, Chuck," Dr. Jillium said, and a flicker of annoyance rose and fell in Meg at the woman's grateful satisfaction. "I was afraid that her recent progress was only a front. I thought her picture might shake the truth from her."

It did, Meg tried to say, but the thought never reached her lips.

"Can you get her back to her room?"

"Yep." Meg felt her head loll as Chuck shifted her weight. "That is an amazing painting," he said, his deep voice rumbling through Meg. "She really did it?"

"Yes. It's like nothing I've ever seen," Dr. Jillium said, and Meg tried to laugh, the sound coming out as a rasping gurgle. She'd get out of here. She had to. Rorry was waiting. He'd take her with him. Dr. J had tricked her with the picture, but she'd be smarter next time. Maybe she and

Christopher could escape together, and then she'd leave him in some alley to find Perfection alone.

"I've always said that it's only the most troubled and imperfect of us that can make the most perfect things," Chuck said as he carried her back to her room.

And Meg, vowing to keep her big mouth shut next time, agreed.